THE ARK OF THE PEOPLE

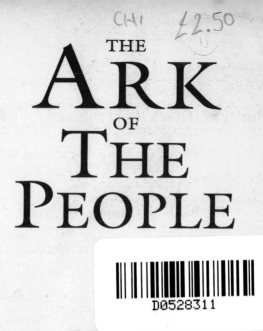

Born in Warwickshire, England, W.J. Corbett joined the Merchant Navy as a galley-boy when he was sixteen and saw the world. Now living in Birmingham, his first book, *The Song of Pentecost*, won the prestigious Whitbread Award.

'Mr Corbett has wit, originality and economy with words which put him straight in the very top class of all . . . beside the authors of such classics as *The Wind in the Willows*, *The Jungle Book* and *Black Beauty*.'

Auberon Waugh, *Daily Mail*

THE
ARK
OF
THE
PEOPLE

W.J. Corbett

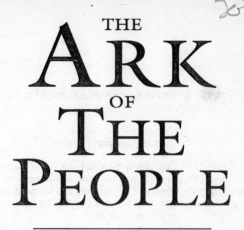

Illustrated by
Wayne Anderson

Hodder
Children's
Books

a division of Hodder Headline plc

Text copyright © 1998 W.J. Corbett
Illustrations copyright © 1998 Wayne Anderson

First published in Great Britain in 1998
by Hodder Children's Books

The right of W.J. Corbett to be identified as the Author
of the Work and the right of Wayne Anderson to be
identified as the illustrator of the work has been asserted
by them in accordance with the Copyright, Designs and
Patents Act 1988.

10 9 8 7 6 5 4 3 2 1

A Catalogue record for this book is available from the
British Library

ISBN 0340 69965 5

Typeset by Palimpsest Book Production Limited,
Polmont, Stirlingshire

Printed and bound in Great Britain by
Mackays of Chatham PLC, Chatham, Kent

Hodder Children's Books
A Division of Hodder Headline plc
338 Euston Road
London NW1 3BH

Contents

One

TWO OAKS AND A STREAM

Long ago when the high hills and the deep valleys were young the People were born. Afraid of the Humans, who stalked and fought on the earth below, they made their homes in secret places. Many set up life in the oak-trees that grew vigorously throughout the land. As time passed they befriended and came to live in harmory with the

1

birds and the small animals who also sought shelter in the world of the trees.

The People were not all of a gentle nature. Centuries before, they had split into often warring clans, each group living separate and different lives. But good or bad, all clans could boast that they belonged to the People. For countless generations, the Willow Clan had lived in their huge spreading oak overhanging the stream, with their friends the birds and animals. It was mostly a good life. The abundance of the seasons provided all of their needs. The fresh rain dripping into the ancient hollows of the boughs formed pools to draw water from, offering cool delight when the weather was hot and one needed a dip. Around the pools grew clumps of herbs and bushes bearing fragrant leaves and delicious berries, mostly seeded by the beaks of the birds who came for a drink and a bathe.

Though they feared the earth below, the Willow Clan adored the beautiful plants that grew on the forest floor. In the dark hours while the feared

Humans were sleeping, they would steal down from their tree to fill bark baskets with rich soil, bulbs and cuttings, and scamper back to plant out their gardens high above the world. As a result, their home bloomed with daffodils, marigolds, purple daisies in the autumn, and green and red holly in winter. Their love for the beauties of nature was such that they named their children after favourite plants.

The clan collected and stored acorns. These they dried and ground into a fine flour to bake into delicious bread. There were also lots of tasty fungi growing on damp patches of bark to add flavour to their vegetable stews. In peaceful times it was bliss to live in their oak, so high above the troublesome world, but they liked the peace to be shattered by certain sounds. They enjoyed the morning and evening chorus when the sun was rising or setting. There were glorious moments in the velvet darkness when the drab nightingales matched their songs against each other. At such times the contented Willow Clan would

3

gaze up at the stars and make a wish upon them.

They wore rough tunics and hose of green or brown, the better to blend into their tree home. They were small people, though some were angry to be classed so. The larger ones boasted that they were almost as tall and as round as the frogs who croaked in the stream below their tree. The clan members could be said to look very much alike, as peas in a pod. This also was greeted with fury by some. Perhaps most did have large brown eyes and snub noses, but the rebels insisted that every clan member was different in some small way. This was true. It was evident in their smiles. Every Willow Clan member had a personal smile totally his or her own. Because the Willow Clan smiled a lot, it was easy to tell who was who.

The clan were skilled carpenters. With their cleverly invented tools, they had hewn and chipped into the trunk and the boughs of their oak to fashion rooms and galleries, and even a quiet library where they could browse through the old books that detailed their long history. For cosiness when winter came, they had sap-burning lanterns to cheer the gloom, plus small fireplaces by which to warm themselves while their pots of stew simmered on the blazing wood-chips. Then, when their stomachs were full, the clan would engage in their favourite pastime of good-natured argument. It didn't matter what they bickered about. It was the whole clan talking and sharing thoughts that was important.

'Why is this oak tree the whole of our world?' asked little Coltsfoot, puzzled. 'I've looked out through our branches lots of times and there's plenty more trees to be seen. And the forest floor below is so temptingly green, but we small ones are forbidden to tread it. Yet you grown-ups creep about it, gathering soil and flowers to make our gardens flourish. I don't believe the Humans are as fierce as you keep telling us. Even giants are capable of kindness. Me and my friends are fed up with being penned up in our oak when there are so many exciting things happening on the earth below. Why can't we venture down in the daylight to judge things for ourselves?'

'We're only allowed to play in the stream that flows beneath the Great Bough,' argued Meadow-sweet. 'Floating around on bits of driftwood can be very boring sometimes. It's always the same. You're whirled a little way on the thrilling ripples and then you have to paddle back because the lunchtime stew is ready.'

'Which always happens in the middle of an adventure,' complained little Dog-rose, an admired explorer. 'Who needs nourishing stew while dis-covering and mapping wonders quite new? After-wards, perhaps, but not in the grip of amazement.'

'Eat up your stew and be quiet,' said his mother, ladling him a steaming bowl, from which he greedily slurped then licked dry.

'The squirrels in our oak romp the earth in daylight,' said Foxglove. She was known for being calm and thoughtful, 'and they always come safe home. If they can sink their toes in the delicious green below, then why can't we?'

'Enough from you, unwise ones,' said Old Elder from his smoky corner by the fire. 'This oak is our world and the stream is our road. It has always been so. And that's enough for you to know. If we were created to live on the earth how could we be the People? Our squirrels, who are quick and nimble, can dodge the Humans who roar and clash the whole day through, but we of the People aren't blessed with such speed. Once caught on the earth we'd be quickly destroyed. Young ones, be thankful for the safe lives you have and don't yearn for things that will only bring you pain and misery.'

'A secure and a happy life is ours,' agreed Grandma Willow, stirring her pot of mushroom stew. 'We've the morning sun to greet our eyes, the night-time moon to soothe them, plus hearty meals at proper times and herbs to make them wholesome.'

'As long as we stay close to our tree and our stream, no harm will come to us,' agreed her husband, Old Elder. 'Ignore this advice and the

People will perish. I say this as your old leader who has read every word of wisdom in the great books in our library.'

'Talking about libraries,' said little Meadowsweet, standing up. 'I have a poem.'

Almost everyone groaned. Meadowsweet was very nice but she did have a pushy way with her poems.

Old Elder sternly silenced them. 'The Willow Clan have always loved a poem,' he said, sucking on his acorn pipe, 'and young Meadowsweet is gifted, I've heard.'

Meadowsweet was eager to oblige. In a breathless rush, she said, 'You won't like it, but I think you will.' Then, standing full-square in the smoky gallery, she launched into her poem, her flashing brown eyes daring anyone to interrupt.

> *'I think I'd be amazed to see*
> *A tree as lovely as our oak*
> *A tree that's full of acorns green*
> *A tree with roots and . . .'*

And then she faltered.

'That's lovely, dear,' said her mother, clapping her hands. 'Finish it, darling, please do. We're all agog to hear how it ends. Don't worry about the rhyming. None of the famous poets in our history books could put a decent rhyme together.'

'I can't think of any more words,' wept Meadowsweet. 'I can't sleep at night worrying about the ends of my poems. The bright colours of millions of words make my head spin.'

'And so your mind should spin,' said her mother, loyally. 'When your brain soars above everyone else's, you're bound to get a headache.'

'Well, in my opinion that was a rubbish poem,' said a rival poet. His name was Teasel. He looked scornfully at the sobbing Meadowsweet. 'I can make a poem that's both beautiful and rhyming. I'll say it, and everyone will love it. Hold on to your stew spoons in case you tremble with emotion.'

'I think I'd be quite stunned to wake,

> *To see more beauty than a drake*
> *A duck whose beak is poised to scoop*
> *Up Meadowsweet in one swift swoop . . .'*

'Teasel does it on purpose,' wailed Meadowsweet, burying her face in her mother's lap. 'He always makes fun of my poems. Tell him to stop, please.'

'I think that's enough poetry for tonight,' said Old Elder, hurriedly. 'Perhaps it's time we all went to bed. We need to be up early in the morning. There are acorns to store and fruits to be picked. And sharp on the dot after midday we need to meet with the squirrel leaders, who are protesting about their bathing rights in the pools. They claim they are being victimised because of their long tails. They are demanding that the problem is thrashed out.'

'Splashed out, more like,' said Robin, a rising young star in the clan. 'Let's be honest, when the squirrels plunge into the pools they wash every-one out with the flicking of their huge tails.'

'The squirrels do cause a lot of waves,' nodded

10

Fern. She was the clever granddaughter of Old Elder, smoking his pipe by the fire. 'Everyone likes swimming with squirrels as friends, but when they lash their furry tails the water boils and we find ourselves high and dry on the shore. I suggest that at the meeting tomorrow they should be reminded of the swimming room their tails take up. In a kindly way, of course. They can't help having tails twice as long as they need to be.'

'Everything will be thrashed out tomorrow,' promised Old Elder. 'And now let us all go to bed to dream of good things and hope that the sun will rise as always in the morning.'

Soon after, the whole of the Willow Clan were tucked up in their hollows in the great oak, and dreaming. But some dreams are always nightmares. For the Willow Clan had enemies they could not forget for too long. Not only the Humans who clashed and smashed on the earth below, but enemies who lived downstream in another oak, where the waters curled like a snake around the bend. These enemies also belonged to the People,

made them hard, in contrast to the Willow Clan whom they despised as soft. Over the generations, the warning creaks and groans and shedding branches from their oak were ignored. It was just a place to sleep and sprawl around, while they plotted their next raid against the Willow Clan. Yet, like all of the People, they also feared to venture to the earth below, where the Humans prowled and bellowed their hatred at each other. Just like their gentle cousins, the oak was their fort, the stream flowing by was their road.

Fearing Human bullies, they were bullies themselves. When a raid was on, they would board their cruelly-harnessed water-vole slaves and sail off on a mission of plunder. The gentle Willow Clan suffered much from the Nightshade Clan's surprise attacks. No appeals from Old Elder and the angry young could prevent them from stealing sacks of acorn flour, dried fruits and herbs, and other vital things. Back in their oak they would laugh and gorge themselves, and recount their bloody deeds. They didn't care at all that their tree was crumbling away, bit by bit, the rotten debris of its once mighty state being whirled away on the racing current of the stream.

They would notice, but too late. Events would soon sweep over them to mock their fierce way of life, with a fury they could not imagine. Then what would they do, the dreaded Nightshade Clan? But, for the moment, they were content to enjoy their stolen booty. If peril lay in the future, why should they care? The future was always so very far ahead . . . they thought.

There was another clan living in the vicinity of the valley. They were a branch of the People shrouded in mystery. They were known as the Fisher Clan and were said to live deep in the bowèls of the earth to avoid the Humans. Legend said that they worshipped a mighty river and cast spells on all strangers who dared to venture into their underground world. But it was all rumour, even when it was whispered that the Fisher Clan had pink eyes and webbed feet, for no one could swear to having seen one of those strange people. So they remained the stuff of childish nightmare and a threat that tired mothers used when their children misbehaved. 'If you don't stop doing that, the Fisher Clan will get you,' they would warn. 'You'll be dragged to their caves and popped in their pots and boiled for supper . . .'

But whether they lived in trees or caves, all belonged to the race known as the People. There would always be that bond between them, no matter how different their lifestyles or the distance between them . . .

Two

A TRICKLE OF BLUE

The magpie lived in a scruffy pile of twigs at the top of the oak tree. It was he who would soon wing alarming news to the sleeping Old Elder. For the moment he was content to sit and admire the morning. Tucked into the nest beside his dozing mate and chick was a small hoard of shiny things he had collected to brighten up their home. There was a paper-clip, some coloured beads from a broken necklace, two odd earrings, plus a few ring-tops from fizzy-drink cans. Contented that his family were full of food he had gathered before dawn, he climbed on to the side of his nest and surveyed the long, deep valley.

Almost at once he spied something interesting. Way down at the end of the valley he saw a beautiful blue object, twisting and glinting in the early sun. His greedy heart raced as he stared. The object was easily the most desirable trinket he had ever seen. Using his binocular vision, he zoomed in for a close-up. Disappointment came: it was just a cascade of water falling into the valley from the hills above. Even as he watched, the blue flow became a muddy brown torrent, and its faint roar could be heard from even this far away. Confused, and suddenly afraid, the bird flapped down from his high perch and poked his head inside the sleeping quarters of his friend, Old Elder.

'Clan leader,' he croaked, rousing him. 'Come quickly and look. Our valley is being flooded with water. It can't be a storm, for there isn't a cloud in the sky!'

Old Elder sighed. He climbed out of his comfy bed, stretched and yawned. He hoped this wasn't a flight of fancy, for the magpie was prone to them. The bird's beady eyes were apt to over-magnify sometimes. But better safe than sorry, Old Elder mused to himself. Soon he was puffing and climbing through the branches of the oak in the wake of the hovering bird.

At the top he sat on the side of the magpie's nest to get his breath back. His sleepy eyes gazed out at a view that had always moved his heart: the long valley emerging from darkness into light in a riot of changing colour, of blues and greens and tawny browns and the purple blush of autumn.

'There, at the head of the valley,' cried the impatient bird. 'What I thought was a precious gem is now a raging brown sludge. And it's getting worse as I speak. What does it mean? What can we do?'

Old Elder gazed, fear rising. Many times, over

the years, he had seen the stream and the valley swollen with rain and burdened with snow. But this was different. As leader of the Willow Clan, he sprang into action. He spoke urgently to his anxious friend, who was poised with open and ready wings on the side of the untidy nest. 'Fly at once,' he ordered. 'Go and rouse Sedge, the water-vole, and tell him to moor beneath the Great Bough that hangs over the stream. Tell him that the lives of everyone in the valley are at stake. Soar speedily now. Meanwhile, I'll hurry down and wake the clan.'

The early risers in the hollows below had sensed that something was amiss. They could hear for themselves the distant roar of water that was disturbing the usual quiet of their valley. When Old Elder returned they gathered to hear what news he might have. Robin and Fern headed the group.

'What's happening Grandfather?' asked Fern, seeing his worried face. 'We saw you scrambling to the top of the tree with the magpie. Is it anything to do with the roaring sound we can hear? Are we being attacked by the Nightshade Clan again?'

'We demand to know, Old Elder,' said Robin, looking his leader in the eye. 'You shared our troubles when we were small, now let us share the troubles that you face in your old age.'

'There are not enough facts to share as yet,' said Old Elder, shaking his grizzled head. 'I only know that water is pouring into the valley from the hills above. It could mean much, or it could mean little. I intend to go and investigate. Sedge will be waiting in the stream to ferry me downstream where I can see things for myself.'

'*We*'ll see things for *our*selves,' corrected Robin. 'For I'm going too. You'll have to sail past the oak of the Nightshade Clan on your journey to the far end of the valley. You'll need a strong right arm if those villains attack you and Sedge. I insist on being that strong right arm.'

'And I'm going too,' said Fern, her brown eyes shining bright. 'I may not be as strong as the charming Robin, who's always flashing his good looks, but my tongue is as sharp as any sword. If the Nightshade Clan attack, I'll lash and shame them with my scolding. I'll beat into their thick skulls that we are on a journey to find out why the brown waters are flooding into our valley. I'll point out that the valley is as much their home as ours, thus the future of all.'

'I can't take others into danger with me,' said Old Elder, though moved by their bravery. 'As your leader I must face alone whatever awaits. And there's Sedge to consider. Could his back cope with the weight of three as opposed to one? He could well sink bubbling to the bottom of the stream beneath the weight of such a tripled burden.'

'I don't agree,' said Fern. 'Sedge has always kept himself fit, and his back is roomy and strong. If the three of us squashed together on his shoulders he would feel no weight at all. And, knowing his sense of humour, he'd only joke about having lumbago because he hadn't got it.'

'If Sedge can joke about three on his back, then why not four?' argued little Coltsfoot, pushing his way to the fore. 'I'm coming along too to fight the Nightshade Clan and frown at the rushing brown waters.'

'Sedge once told me that five was his favourite number,' piped Meadowsweet. She explained, though no one believed her, 'Last week he was a bit glum so to cheer him up I shouted, "Five!" at him, which made him roll over and over in the stream with mirth. He gasped that he'd never been so tickled in all his life. So I'm coming on the expedition too. Sedge might need someone to shout, "Five!" in his ear if he gets all glum again.'

'You two will stay at home,' said Old Elder, wagging a stern finger at Coltsfoot and Meadowsweet. 'Go and join Teasel, who plans to study poetry in the library today. You might even come up with a good rhyme between you.'

Coltsfoot and Meadowsweet turned and slunk off to obey, bitterly disappointed.

'Which leaves the correct number,' said Robin, happily. 'Three of the Willow Clan will be journeying down the stream to meet the enemy and the dashing waters head on. I'll go and string my bow,' and off he ran.

'Weapons never solve problems,' said Fern, scornfully. 'The so-called handsome Robin is just trying to impress me as usual. I'm ready to travel immediately, Grandfather. If we hurry we'll leave Robin twanging his bow in anger while we sail off on the back of Sedge.'

With the magpie hovering above, the two left the meeting-hall in the Great Bough. This mighty limb, which hung over the stream, was enshrined in the long history of the clan. It contained a warren of hollows where endangered folk could hide from their enemies, plus stores of food in case of siege. It was almost a holy place, filled with mystery and legend. Here, in its comforting, quiet places, the Willow Clan came to express grief or happiness.

Sedge the water-vole got up as the pair came

clambering down the bough to where its twigs trailed in the water. He had been lying on his back, exercising his paws and tail to get in trim for the long, downstream journey the magpie had warned him to expect. Seeing Old Elder, he winked a spray-filled eye.

'Sedge, faithful friend,' said the oldster. 'The magpie has told you about the dangers we all face with the waters rushing into our valley?'

'I'm fully aware,' nodded Sedge, 'and I'm ready to do my duty to save us all.'

'But there's a problem,' said Old Elder, awkwardly. 'My granddaughter and Robin, the impetuous youth, insist on coming along. I'm worried about how much weight your back can bear.'

'Let me worry about that,' replied the confident Sedge. 'If I develop lumbago later in life it's all in a good cause. Come, climb aboard, let's go see what threat this torrent poses for our valley. And don't warn me about having to pass the oak of the Nightshade Clan – I know them as well as you do.'

'Let's cast off quickly,' said Fern, settling herself between Sedge's ears. 'Before that boastful Robin turns up with his bow and arrows.'

Her plea was too late. At that moment, Robin came racing down the Great Bough and jumped aboard.

'Oh, we were afraid we'd left you behind,' lied Fern. 'Settle near Sedge's tail where you'll be out of the way. And don't flex your bow while we're sailing and steering, you'll only fall overboard.'

With the three secure on his back, Sedge swam out into the middle of the stream to take advantage of the current that would help them on their way. As they came nearer the bend in the stream and the oak of the Nightshade Clan, all four became quieter. But their resolve never faltered. The threat to the valley was more important than the threat to their personal safety. Even now the rush of dirty brown water was louder in their ears . . .

The magpie, winging above, was keeping a sharp look-out for danger and treasure. His lust

Three

PERIL ON THE STREAM

'Why, if it isn't Old Elder,' jeered a voice from a branch above. It was Chief Deadeye, the leader of the Nightshade Clan – so named because he had lost an eye during a vicious battle. He sneered, 'And I see he's brought two suckpaps along to boost his courage. So, what brings you here, Old Elder? Come slumming, have you? Come to beg us not to raid you so often? Or have you come to study our table manners? Well, we've got none and proud of it. So you can turn that ferry slave round and sail back to your flowery tree.'

The gang in the branches around him sniggered. They enjoyed it when Deadeye lashed out with his nasty tongue.

'This is no time for turning round,' shouted Old Elder, standing on Sedge's back, urgency in his tone. 'Please listen, Deadeye. There's a torrent of water flooding into the head of the valley and we're on our way to investigate. Let us pass in peace. Though you and your gang have made our clans enemies, we still all belong to the People. What disaster we find at the head of the valley will affect us all.'

His answer was a hail of arrows that zipped into the water around Sedge. They were teasing arrows just meant to frighten. However, a single spear spun lazily in the air to tear through the water-vole's ear. It had been thrown by Hemlock, the odious son of Deadeye. He was lounging against a bough, surrounded by his giggling friends. Then, like the coward he was, he melted out of sight. Sedge whimpered with pain but he didn't buckle. He bravely remained on an even keel to protect his passengers.

'How could you harm our friend?' cried Fern, rushing forward to tend Sedge's ear. 'You've enjoyed your taste of blood, now let us go.'

'You ignore my flood warning and now you injure Sedge,' shouted Old Elder, angrily. 'And how many times have you invaded our oak and stolen our stores, leaving misery and carnage behind? Do you only live for bloodshed and mayhem? Shame on you, Nightshade Clan!'

'Your Sedge is only a common ferrier,' called Chief Deadeye, scornfully. 'Water-voles are for using until they drop dead from exhaustion. When one dies, you can always harness up another. You call him 'friend'? Well, that word doesn't appear in the violent history books of our clan.'

'That's because you've never had friends!' shouted Fern. 'How I wish we had a strong champion among our clan to put you in your place.'

'But you haven't,' sneered Deadeye. 'Now prepare for the next shower of arrows, stupid gatherers of flowers. This time we'll aim true.'

The words were barely out of his mouth when the arrow struck. Yelling with shock and pain, Deadeye found himself pinned by the ear to a branch. While his crawling cronies rushed to free him, the rest of the Nightshade Clan stared down at the stream in amazement.

The sight they saw was Robin, balancing on Sedge's tail and calmly notching another arrow to his bow. 'If blood is your argument, then argue with me!' he yelled. 'In the absence of the craven son, the father pays for his sin. Loose off your arrows, Nightshade Clan. But be sure to kill me before my quiver empties, for every shaft will take one of your wicked lives. But we can settle this quarrel with two arrows. Let Hemlock step into the open with his bow. He can fire the first arrow. If he misses I will shoot. So where is your

31

brave son, Deadeye? Has he courage enough to take up my challenge?'

There was a lot of scurrying about in the branches above. The anxious expedition below had to wait some time before a worried-looking ruffian arrived to call down to them, 'Our champion Hemlock says he's thirsting to fight the upstart Robin Prettyface,' he lied, 'but he can't find his bow and arrows anywhere. He's hunting all over the place but can't remember where he put them. He swears that when he does find them he'll fill you so full of arrows that you'll look like hedgehogs.'

'Some champion,' scoffed Robin. 'Send out a dozen of your fighters and I will shock them. Or you can tell Hemlock to forget his bow and arrows and come down to the stream and we'll fight with sword or stave, I don't mind.'

'Hemlock's having a snooze at the moment,' came the embarrassed reply. 'All the dashing about searching for his bow and arrows has made the blood rush to his head and tired him out. But he vows that as soon as he wakes up he'll be ready to fight you in mortal combat, Pretty Robinface.'

It was a backing down of the most cowardly sort. The worried magpie, fluttering above, looped the loop for joy. Sedge grinned through his pain, proud to have a hero balancing on his tail. Fern was filled with admiration for the one she had dismissed as merely handsome, though she kept it to herself.

As for Old Elder, he felt as though a great burden had been lifted from his tired shoulders. Now he knew who would succeed him as leader of the Willow Clan when his time was over. He called again up into the branches of the oak. 'So, can we now pass without hindrance? On our return from the head of the valley, I hope we can speak again in peace about the flood that could threaten all our lives. Let's hope it's a false alarm and we can bring good news. But if the news is bad, we must face the crisis together, Chief Deadeye, for we all belong to the People. If the valley and the lives of our clans are at stake, the problems we face will not be solved with bows and arrows.'

'Tell Hemlock I'll shake his hand in friendship if our clans unite to fight the flood together,' said Robin, generously. 'I don't much relish having to shoot an arrow through his wicked heart, for as a member of the Willow Clan peace is my goal.'

'I'll mention it to him,' was the ruffian's grudging reply. 'That's if he's woken up.'

'I'll have you one day, Robin Prettyface,' snarled a muffled voice from inside the tree. 'You'll regret making me look a fool in front of the gang. Go and worry about your trickles of water, we don't care. Go and fret about everything while we fret about nothing. But fret seriously about one thing, sworn enemy. When I rise from my bed and find my bow and arrows, there'll be one less strutting Robin in this valley.'

His brave words were heartily cheered by the relieved gang members, who had begun to lose faith in Hemlock, their champion fighter.

'And don't think Hemlock's words are idle

rise of water. The evidence was everywhere. Clumps of high-riding lily-pads and watercress had been torn from their roots and now lolled forlornly in the ugly brown wash. Waves lapped at the homes of kingfishers and small crawling creatures, causing much distress. An otter with a silver fish in his whiskered jaws sat on a favourite dry stone in the stream, puzzled to notice that his toes were being lapped by scummy ripples. What had always been a thread of clear water through a valley was fast becoming a spreading lake.

Sedge was tiring visibly as he battled against the onrushing water. His courage stirred Robin and Fern to action. Slipping from his back they swam alongside, their fingers tugging at his fur to help him along. Old Elder, sitting alone, felt quite helpless. If he could have turned back the years he would have been beside those three in their brave battle against the waves. But he was old and his bones would never again respond to his wishes. Yet, though sad, he felt some contentment, for he was confident that the future would be safe in those two pairs of hands helping Sedge plough through the water.

The magpie, flying scout above, also wished he could do more to help. He could only show his devotion by yelling, 'In, out . . . in . . . out,' to Sedge and the breast-stroking swimmers alongside him. It didn't matter if his coxing sometimes broke their rhythm, for the three in the water knew he was doing his best.

Then, suddenly, they had reached the head of the valley, a scene of crashing chaos and whipped foam. The ugly sight made their senses reel. The violently disturbed air seemed to tear the breath from their throats. Exhausted and despairing, the expedition gazed through stinging eyes at the catastrophe that would surely destroy their beloved valley.

'It's the work of the Humans,' cried Old Elder above the howling wind. 'They've built a dam of stone piled on stone and now they've released the waters to form a new sea. This heralds the death knell of our valley, my children. Let us turn back while there's still time, before we're smashed to pieces. We must hurry home and raise the alarm.'

There were few more words, the effort and their emotions solely concerned with leaving this terrible place as quickly as possible. As if to mock their grief and anger a rainbow formed above the ugly cascade, its beauty offering not hope but destruction. Sedge swirled in the water and headed for home.

Hours later, the silent expedition was coasting into calmer waters that carried only a tinge of dirty foam as warning of the deluge to come. The peace and quiet was balm to their distressed minds. They rested to collect their thoughts, Robin fuming, Fern softly weeping. The magpie, fluttering above Sedge's nose, shook his head in sadness, while the brave water-vole sighed deeply into his drooping whiskers. Meanwhile, Old Elder sat and pondered deeply as all good leaders do in times of crisis.

The heron fishing in the stream seemed blithely

unaware of the approaching calamity that would soon destroy his way of life. He had raised his beak haughtily to stare at the bedraggled expedition as it coasted into his shallows. Then he appeared to shrug his wings as he returned to the serious business of spearing silver fish. They had always been plentiful in this stretch of the stream, so the bird had few cares in the world. He was only a mite concerned to notice that the once clear waters were clouding. But being a proud fisher of fishes, he took on the challenge, for with his deft skills he could spear silver fish with his eyes tight shut.

Having rested, the expedition continued its homeward journey. Old Elder still sat deep in thought on Sedge's undulating back. Questions were racing through his mind. How long would it take for the waters to burst from the deep basin below the dam and roar unchecked down the stream? How could the Willow Clan fight such a mighty force as they attempted to save themselves? Then a germ of an idea began to form in his mind: an idea that might save the cruising down the stream, on your sunshine day out, for he'll need them.'

'Why do we talk of fighting?' asked Old Elder, wearily. 'We have just returned from the head of the stream where we witnessed the beginning of the end of our world as we know it. If only I could make you understand the perils that face us all.'

'Don't waste your words, Grandfather,' cried Fern. 'This wicked clan will never heed good advice until it's too late.'

'Before what's too late?' said Deadeye, dimly. 'No one can accuse my clan of being late for anything. You lot should know how early my gang arrives when we raid your tree. Why, you're only just climbing out of bed when we've already pinched your stores and kicked everything over. That's what being too late means.'

At this point, Robin intervened again. From his battle position on Sedge's tail, he shouted up, 'Old Elder is trying to save your lives, if you'll only listen to his wisdom. But if you choose to insult him, then insult me instead. I've made my challenge, and here is my breast and here I strut. As Hemlock has finished skulking, perhaps he would like to try to shoot an arrow through my heart. Or is he like all cowards, all sound and fury, signifying nothing? So step from the shadows, craven Hemlock, or for ever hold your tongue.'

Fern was thrilled to hear yet more words of courage from Robin. She was pleased that she could admire him not only for his handsome looks but for his stout defence of them all. Yet her heart went out to him as she gazed: he looked so slight and vulnerable, standing there on Sedge's tail, prepared to give his life for their small, floating party. But, then, true heroes didn't always bulge with muscles, she thought.

Suddenly a figure appeared from behind a screen of browning autumn leaves. It was Hemlock, who had been shaken awake by his worried friends and presented with his lost bow and arrows. He looked ugly and confident, with good reason. Around him crowded his cronies, all armed to the teeth and prepared to hurl themselves in front of an arrow aimed at his heart. For the ruffians, in their simple minds, reasoned that if Hemlock was lost, who would lead them when Chief Deadeye had passed away? Feeling safe amid numbers, Hemlock began to stalk up and down the bough, doing what he did best, namely bragging and boasting.

'Tremble at the sight of me, Robin Goodness,' he bawled. 'You know by now my name is Hemlock. And my ambition is to kill in cold blood a certain someone who is too handsome for his own good!'

'And without the help of his bodyguards too!' cried Chief Deadeye, hopefully. 'On his own, my brave son will prove more than a match for the puny Robin.'

'So, what are you waiting for, Hemlock?' yelled Robin. 'Climb down from your tree and fight me. Or will you send your ruffian friends to do your dirty work? Meet me in the shallows of this stream with bow, with sword or stave. Just come alone, for only a coward fights behind the protection of others.'

Perhaps it was a sign of anger from Heaven. Perhaps it was a simple warning from the black clouds gathering above the surging flood at the head of the valley. Whatever the cause, a furious storm broke over the land, torrents of rain lashing down as the clouds released their load. Then came one mighty roll of thunder followed by a single bolt of lightning. The brightness of the flash seared the eyes of the awed watchers. The power of the bolt struck the trunk of the Nightshade oak, leaving it burning and sagging more than ever. The sudden fury of it had sent Hemlock and his ruffians scurrying for safety into their hollowed dens. Then, as quickly as it had started, the storm passed. The evening sun ruled the sky again as it slid, brightly orange, behind the hills.

'So much for the champion Hemlock,' said Robin, contemptuously. 'Fierce with words, yet terrified by rain and a single lightning flash.'

'What a pity the lightning struck the tree,'

said Fern, 'instead of the cowardly Hemlock's backside.'

'Deadeye,' shouted Old Elder, 'perhaps the lightning strike on your oak should be taken as a sign. I appeal to you one last time. Let us join our clans together and work out a plan to save all the People before the floods arrive, for arrive they surely will.'

'The hardy Nightshade Clan have no use for plans,' sneered Deadeye. 'The only plans we discuss are how to storm your tree and steal all your stores before you've even rubbed the sleep from your eyes. So sail back to your tree and worry yourself sick about the future. Me and my clan intend to carry on as usual. If the flood comes, then it comes. The Nightshade Clan will survive somehow. And another thing, as my son Hemlock dashed out of the rain he was heard to mutter that when the weather dries up he will destroy your Robin Goodfellow, once and for all. My Hemlock always wins battles on dry days.'

'Tell Hemlock he'll have a dry mouth when we meet,' shouted Robin. 'And when my dart goes through his heart he'll have only dry eyes to mourn him.'

'I'll tell him what you said, don't fret,' raged Deadeye. 'Just dread the day when he stuffs your boasts back down your throat.'

'Why do you defend your cowardly son?' cried Fern. 'Here is Robin soaking wet while Hemlock skulks in a dry bolt-hole.'

'Get back to your cooking pots, impudent wench!' yelled Deadeye. 'You should be at home in the kitchen, stirring stew, instead of poking your nose into war.'

Seeing that Fern was about to explode, Old Elder gently restrained her. 'He's not worth your anger, my child. We've wasted too much time in argument. We need to get home to prepare the clan for the dangers they face.'

'May I anticipate your next order, Old Elder?' said Sedge, wincing from the pain of his stiffening ear. 'The order that is the wish of us all?'

'You may,' smiled the oldster. 'That order being to flip your paws and tail for home. And full speed ahead, if you can manage it.'

'Delighted to oblige,' grinned Sedge, spinning round in the water and surging at full throttle towards home and kin, and all things wonderfully familiar.

'Home!' cried the magpie, happily winging on the way. 'My chick has probably learned to fly while I've been away protecting this expedition. I wouldn't be surprised if he flew out to meet me.'

Meanwhile, the Nightshade gang had emerged from hiding after their stormy fright. They were experts at being brave when danger had passed. Lounging among the branches of their still smoking tree, they jeered and sneered at full voice until the expedition disappeared from view around the bend in the stream.

During that homeward lap Old Elder once again pondered the idea he had had to save his clan from the waters when they arrived.

Before the party reached home he had a firm plan. A plan that would depend for success on co-operation and speed of action. He was sure he could command both.

Soon the tired expedition was cruising in to moor beneath the Great Bough. They were immediately hailed as heroes by the waiting gathering, who rushed joyfully to help them ashore. Sedge, with his bloody ear, was patted and cheered when it was learned how he had acquired his wound. The proud magpie was congratulated on his first-class scouting job. In their innocence, the Willow Clan knew little about the terrible danger they would be facing in the hours to come. They would shortly find out . . .

Later that night the culprits who had caused the flooding of the valley would be peacefully asleep. They knew nothing about the People who lived in the oaks and in other secret places because of their fear of the Humans. Such ridiculous ideas were dismissed as folklore and myth. Though there were moments in sleep, when they saw the small people clearly. During restless nights such ancient memories disturbed them and made them start. Then came the blessed day and the first rays of the sun to sweep away their fears . . .

Four

AND THERE WERE GIANTS
TOO . . .

Long ago, when the same high hills and the deep valleys were formed, the Humans were born. Fearful of the spirits and the magical small people they believed lived in the dark forests, they made their homes in the sunlit uplands. As time passed, they came to live in a harmony of sorts with the dogs and wild horses, which helped them in their hunt for the deer, and the ox that provided their food and clothing.

They were not very gentle, the Human people. Many centuries before, they had split into tribes and fought bloody battles to decide who were the stronger. Yet as they slew their fellow man they were loud in their boast that they all belonged to the Human race.

For thousands of years they had wandered the plains and hills, following the wild herds. Some tribes broke away from that restless life to plant seeds in the earth, to harvest food for themselves and their animal companions. From this static way of life came a village that grew into a town and then a city. The elders of these tribes became rich and powerful. Controlling the harvests and the herds they became kings and lords and holy men. To make their images more mysterious, they claimed kinship with the spirits and the small people who wove spells in the depths of the dark woods and valleys. The holy men declared that, through the knowledge learned while wandering those feared places, they could predict the future.

'Tonight the moon will rise again as it did last night,' proclaimed a holy man. 'This was whispered into my ear by one of the small people as I lay in a trance in the forest.'

The simple Humans gasped in astonishment when his words came true.

'Tomorrow morning the sun will rise as it did yesterday morning,' promised the holy man. 'This was also whispered into my ear.'

His accuracy was so amazing that all remaining doubts were swept away when the sun rose and shone down on a beautiful new day.

Then came a time when a new king was crowned. His chief lord held the crown high and declared, 'This crown was fashioned by the magical people who live in the shades of our world. It is blessed by the spirits with a warning that it may be passed only from father to son. So, let us praise our king who will reign over us for ever more . . .'

The cheers of the simple Humans grew hoarse as the ceremony dragged on and on. In fact, the People who lived in the oaks possessed no magic or spells that could order the world. The People were as ordinary and as down-to-earth as it was possible to be, when one lived in a tree. They would have been bemused had they known that the Humans credited them with such powers.

Many more centuries passed, and the Humans entered a new phase in their history. Like the People who lived in the hollows of trees, they made books about their long heritage that gloried their cleverness and wisdom. They built cathedrals in honour of those they worshipped, built dungeons to hold the ones they feared. But always they fled back to their tribes in times of trouble, eager to fight their enemies in the white heat of argument and anger. Yet the constant clashing of shield and sword could weary even the fiercest as another score was settled in the old bloody way. After each battle they would rest and tend their wounds in the forests and valleys, their cooking fires attracting small creatures that stole from hiding to gaze in curiosity.

Also curious were the People who lived in such places, high in their oaks. In a certain valley, where the trees grew thick and where a stream ran, two clans viewed the Human battles through different eyes.

The Nightshade Clan were enthralled to watch the carnage taking place below their tree. They even chose sides and silently urged on the fighting. When the Humans had left they would ape them in mock battle. But it grew more serious. Soon they were fashioning swords and daggers and bows of slivers torn from their oak. Thus armed, they took to attacking their gentler cousins who lived in nearby trees, who were defenceless against such modern skills. And so the divide among the clans of the People widened into hatred and bewilderment.

The Willow Clan had always been saddened to see the Humans killing each other on the forest floor. They saw the limp dead and listened to the cries of the injured and grieved. What was the point? they thought. Was it some disease the Humans had caught that caused them to fall into madness? Disease it was, for it was rapidly spreading among the People themselves.

The Nightshade Clan had already shattered many times the peace the Willow Clan had enjoyed for so much of their existence . . .

More centuries passed, and the Humans took over the world with their inventions. Ever busy beavers, they built a dam across the head of the long valley that was the ancient home of the trees and flowers and animals . . . and the People.

It had been the magpie, perched on the side of his nest at the top of the oak, who noticed the first beautiful blue trickle . . . Now the expedition had arrived back at the Great Bough with the news confirmed . . .

Five

THE BUILDING OF THE ARK

The Willow Clan had gathered in the meeting-hall of the Great Bough when word came that the expedition was home. Though afraid to hear the worst, their hearts were trusting as Old Elder spoke.

'Many of you know about the waters flooding into our valley,' he began. 'At the head of the valley we discovered a dam built by the Humans. That dam must have been holding back vast amounts of water from the rivers that flow around our valley. Now they have opened the dam and released the water. I can only think that the Humans intend to create a huge lake that will swallow up our homes and most of the surrounding countryside. Though why, I cannot say.'

'Perhaps they are making a pool to draw water from, just as we do,' suggested Grandma Willow. 'Only a pool much larger, they being much larger than us.'

'Perhaps,' Old Elder said. He spoke on urgently. 'But whatever the reason for the flood, I don't need to tell you of the dangers we now face. I've been working out a plan that might save us. I need all to do as I ask without question. First I address the skilled carpenters. Friends, hurry and gather your sharp axes and hammers, all of your wood-working tools, and rush them back here for you have much work to do. In the meantime, everyone else must hurry and gather all precious belongings from the old homes and bring them here. Snatch up everything that might be useful in an emergency. Now, all of you, scurry . . . go!'

No sooner ordered than done, such was the worry and the eagerness of the Willow Clan. As the sun finally set, everyone was busy. There was much dashing through the hollow trunk and branches that had been a secure home for centuries past. The People worked with a will, as they always did when they had complete faith in their leader. The many tasks and errands they carried out that night were lit by smoky lantern and bright moonlight.

The sound of axes and hammers and the flying chips of fresh-cut wood set the main scene for those night-time hours. As the carpenters and other skilled workers toiled to Old Elder's instructions, many more were making haste to strip the oak of every last item that might serve them in an uncertain future. Pots and pans and other personal objects were snatched up to be hurriedly stored in the Great Bough's winding galleries.

The small ones attacked the Great Library and loaded themselves with armfuls of books – for such records would be vital in times to come if they should begin to forget their history. Sitting cross-legged in the flickering light, the weavers wove and stitched their coarse cloth into useful shapes like spare hose and tunics and stout boots. Then in the final hour before the new day, the exhausted People rested. Even the owls had been long a-bed when they closed their eyes in sleep. Now, the only sounds of industry came from the carpenters, who were nearing the end of their huge task. As they toiled to finish before the hour of daybreak, the weather took a vicious turn. The winds began to howl and the surface of the stream to thrash as the force of water dashed against its banks.

'Willow Clan,' shouted Old Elder, walking among the sleeping forms. 'The crucial moment is approaching. Hurry and crowd into the meeting-hall. Be sure that nothing and no one is left behind. Soon you will be hearing loud noises and frightening sounds and violent movement, but don't be afraid. Remember, our clan has survived for so many centuries because of our stout hearts. When you are gathered together, sing songs and tell stories and poems to keep up your courage. We now face the greatest threat to our existence but never will we be reviled as cowards by the People who might survive us.'

He was instantly obeyed. Minutes later, the Willow Clan were packing the meeting-hall singing and telling jokes to mask the awful fear they felt. Old Elder hurried back to where the carpenters were completing their task. He was proud to see Fern and Robin working alongside them. Now he could only pray that his plan would work. At that moment, the chief carpenter gave an urgent nod. This was the signal for everyone to dash for the safety of the meeting-hall.

They were only just in time. As dawn broke, there sounded an enormous groan and the ear-splitting crack of splintering wood. Then followed a violent shuddering and a heart-in-the-mouth plunge. All this ended with an almighty splash and the grinding of pebbles. Then came the light.

While the clan had been busy, so had the waters. The once blue stream was swelling visibly, its surface washed by dirty brown scum. The oak of the Willow Clan had also dramatically changed its appearance. Thanks to the work of the carpenters, the Great Bough that had always spread majestically over the stream had been hacked from its trunk and now lay on the bed of the rising stream. It was a barely moving hulk, but that would change. In the meantime, from the innards of that bulk drifted song and laughter, for words and music always calmed the fearful heart . . .

Having kept a close check on the happenings below, the magpie decided it was time to change his address. He had watched all the hacking and had witnessed the final moment when the Great Bough crashed down to the stream. With a few quick words to his mate and his chick, he went into action. Soon they were flying to and fro with beakfuls of twigs and leaves, which they carelessly built into a new nest in a slender branch a-top the Great Bough. To their chick fell the honour of flying the family treasures to the new home, for those glittering things would one day be his inheritance.

The squirrels and the other oak-dwelling creatures were not slow in coming forward. They speedily set up new headquarters in the branches of the Great Bough that lay like a huge stranded whale among the pebbles of the ever-swelling stream. At last, all the work that could be done to survive had been done. Old Elder's orders had been carried out to the letter. Now all that remained was the waiting and the prayers that went with it. It was all the Willow Clan could do, was all anyone could do.

'Sing up, my children!' cried Old Elder, as the songs trailed away to a murmur. The awful waiting was getting to everyone. He went on, jovially, 'Come, let's live for this time when we're all together. Let the waters crash around us but they'll never dash our hopes for the future.'

'If an old fire goes out, then light a new one,' murmured Grandma Willow, stirring a new stew on a new fire. 'The new stew may taste a bit different but it will taste familiar in time.'

A couple of sturdy youngsters had lugged her black cauldron from the old oak to an emergency kitchen in the Great Bough. As she stirred, she softly crooned an old song that was quickly drowned in a babble of voices.

'I haven't got a new song to sing, but I've made a new poem,' cried Meadowsweet. 'While we're being attacked by nasty water, my poem is about nice water. I know I won't remember every word, but I probably will.' She looked scruffy and tired after hours of stacking precious books into the storehouse of the Great Bough. Though as afraid as anyone, at this moment she refused to let her fear show as she stood on her toes and quoted her poem, closely watched and listened to by her deadly rival Teasel.

'I think that water is quite nice,
I've dipped my toes in once or twice,
Then pulled them out for they were blue,
They blushed back to their pinky hue.
If all your toes stay true to you,
Then you will like nice water too.'

'That poem isn't about water, it's about toes,' scoffed Teasel. He had spent the night sweeping up wood-chips and passing cool water to the sweating carpenters. Though he believed himself to be the greatest poet the Willow Clan had ever bred, he was still proud to know what it felt like to do horny-handed toil. Pushing sobbing Meadowsweet aside, he launched into a cheeky poem he had thought up on the spur of the moment.

'I think that water is quite wet
I've never seen dry water yet
But of the people I have met
Our Meadowsweet must be the wettest yet.'

'Teasel is insulting me again,' wept Meadow-sweet. And just look at him grinning as usual. Why does he always have to spoil things with ugly jokes? If we weren't about to be swamped by the flood, I'd hate him even more than I did yesterday. If we survive, I'm going to get him barred from the Poetry Lovers' Club.'

'I think our brilliant children are beginning to despair about the desperate water situation. Most children get peevish when they can't see a future for themselves,' said a worried oldster, looking for somewhere to knock out his pipe in this new place. 'In my day, poems were about foxgloves and butterflies and true love. Now they write poems about frost-bitten toes and dry water. Where is the beauty in such things? If Teasel survives the flood, I suspect he'll become an arty poet who buries his face in his hands and weeps through his fingers. I just can't understand the lad.'

'There will be no more gloom and doom among this clan,' said Old Elder, sharply. 'This is a time when we must cheer each other up and have faith in ourselves. I can hear the roar of the water getting louder as I speak. Let us join as one and pray that our efforts have not been in vain. We will now sing the happiest song we can think of. For if we're about to die at least we'll die with a tune on our lips as in the best tradition of the Willow Clan.'

Though the clan sang brightly about the glories of sunshine, there was no sun that morning, only angry black clouds packing the sky and winds howling through the branches and hollows of the Great Bough where the Willow Clan, and their animal friends, huddled together for comfort. Then suddenly the terrible long waiting was over . . .

The first great wave arrived, tearing up trees and shrubs by their roots. The old oak tree groaned and swayed before such a force. Timeless hollowing by the clan had weakened its trunk and limbs to resist. Its ancient life was measured in minutes. Embedded in the stream, the Great

Bough lurched before the pressure of the tide, then rose to float free. Its bulk rolled this way and that before settling into a natural sailing mode, heavy side down. At this point Old Elder, Fern and Robin hurried from below to see what was happening up top.

'My dear children,' yelled Old Elder, his joyous words just heard above the lash of spray and the wailing of the wind, 'just as I prayed, the Great Bough is now a ship, an ark to bear us all to safety.'

'So there is hope for us yet, Grandfather,' screamed Fern, clinging to a slender frond as the gale sought to tear her away.

'With our strength and some luck we'll ride out this storm,' shouted Robin, gripping them both with his strong hands. 'No matter how wide the sea of troubles that faces us, one day we'll find a shore and a new valley for us all.'

Then it was back to battle stations as the three went below, encouraging the clan members to brave the awful buffeting and noise and to hang on to their senses and loved ones. Surprisingly, two poets of differing styles had buried their quarrels to comfort the wailing old and the weeping infants, lurching among those in need of soothing words.

Though working tirelessly to help his people, Teasel, because of his teasing nature, had to quip, 'If we survive, Meadowsweet, we'll write an epic poem together about this time.'

'Yes, Teasel, we must,' gasped Meadowsweet, thrilled to the tips of her pink toes. 'When this is all over, our poems should mingle as one.'

'Good. I'll think up the clever words and you can scribble 'em down,' grinned Teasel, as he passed her by. Her furious reply was lost as she moved on to bustle among the distressed clan.

Sedge and his family had been washed from their dry burrow in the bank by that first crashing wave. Being strong swimmers, they easily coped with the surging water. With his wife and bullet-nosed youngsters in tow, the faithful water-vole swam across to the Great Bough, which was now riding high and seaworthy. He and his brood clambered aboard, anxious to offer help.

Then the second wave came roaring in, closely followed by the third. And all at once the green and peaceful valley was no more. As far as the eye could see in any direction was water, and above, a sullen, brooding sky.

'Goodbye, old oak, old home,' murmured Old Elder, mourning to see the roots of the tree tearing from the ground as their refuge of ages fell, amid splintering shrieks, to its death on the forest floor. Then, suddenly, he, Fern and Robin heard plaintive cries from the raging waters below.

'Save us,' the voices implored. 'Our oak is destroyed and many of us are drowned. We implore you, Willow Clan, have mercy on us, the survivors.'

Only a short time earlier the first great wave had struck the already tottering tree of the Nightshade Clan. Long weakened through neglect, it was quickly reduced to driftwood, leaving its clan fighting for their lives in the cold brown water. Clinging to the swirling flotsam of wood, those who survived were swept along on the second wave, some holding desperately to their young ones – for even that wicked clan had some loving souls among its members. Now, here they were, bobbing like corks on the water and begging for help.

For one brief moment, Fern and Robin were tempted to leave them to their fate but were quickly humbled by Old Elder. 'It's not for us to judge between the wicked and the good,' he shouted, above the storm, 'for if we refuse to help them, how will we be judged in some future history of this time?'

Inspired by his words, Fern and Robin set to work. They were joined by Sedge and his family. The water-voles dived continually into the water to load the gasping survivors on to their backs, to offload them into the strong and willing arms of Robin and Fern and the many volunteers from the Willow Clan. It was noted with distaste that

Deadeye and Hemlock his son were amongst the first pleading to be rescued. But the toiling team were glad to snatch the small ones, their mothers and other innocents from their pitiful driftwood rafts. Many lives were saved that terrible morning. Many were the gasped and babbled thanks as other members of the Willow Clan came from below to haul aboard the more exhausted survivors, who were in danger of being swept away from the haven of the Great Bough. Only Deadeye, Hemlock and their hard core of villains refused to be grateful. Though half drowned, they still found the energy to cast murderous glances at the Willow people. Clearly they resented being saved from certain death by the gentle folk they despised for their charitable natures. But this was no time to argue or fight. The saving of all life was important, whether those lives were good or evil . . .

'Take them below and tend them,' ordered Old Elder. He saw the anger in the eyes of Fern and Robin. 'And I mean tend everyone equally. At this time our enemy is not aboard this ark but all around it. Whatever we may think of the Nightshade Clan they still belong to the People. If the flood tried to take their lives we certainly won't, as long as I am leader.'

The sturdy, gentle hands of the Willow Clan carried the shivering wretches below into the dry, warm hollows of the saviour ark. By this time the once Great Bough was indeed beginning to behave like a rudderless ship as it wallowed and turned in aimless circles, everyone trying to find their sea-legs. In the safety from the weather, below deck, the shivering and injured castaways were being warmed and fed and rubbed down with soothing bark oil. True to their code, the Willow Clan refused to see enemies in helpless victims.

In the meantime, the ark continued to buck and rear and circle before the punishing waves. Only when night fell did the fury abate. The waters become calm and the stormy clouds cleared. The moon and the stars dominated the heavens again.

But there were no witnesses to rejoice for, without exception, the shocked people aboard the ark were all below and sleeping the sleep of the utterly spent. Their dreams were scatty and confused, though mostly filled with terror. There was much wailing and shouting in the night as the exhausted were shocked again and again from sleep, as they relived their nightmares of the day. None had time to worry about the new terrors the morning might bring . . .

Six

ADRIFT ON A SILVER SEA

The early risers crawled from their damp bedding and shakily climbed on deck. It was as if the crashing waves and the storms had never been. The scene that greeted their tired gaze was wonderful to behold, if alien to their woodland eyes. Everywhere was the glitter of water. As the sun rose, its beams cast a silver sheen over the calm expanse. Shielding their eyes and peering, the early ones could just make out a faint green smudge that was the land far away. The Great Bough, their saving ark, seemed to be drifting idly towards it.

'It's land, all right, shipmates,' cried the magpie, winging in and perching on a swaying twig. 'And what a sad bit of land it is. Meadows, a few sickly poplars and miles of prickly hedgerows. Not an oak tree to be seen, I'm afraid. But let's keep our beaks up. Where there's one shore there must be another on the opposite side, or the world wouldn't make sense. Unfortunately I didn't have time to search for the twin shore because my chick has been squawking for grubs since first light.'

'If this is an official meeting, then I demand to be present,' said an orange chief squirrel, his tail bristling with temper. He had leaped down from his bed among some twigs high above the deck. He went on, 'My comrades demand to know why they've suddenly become sailors without being consulted. We squirrels also haven't forgot about the swimming-pool argument when we were about to be banned because of the length of our tails.'

'All queries and complaints must wait until Old Elder wakes up after his much-deserved rest,' said the magpie, firmly. 'Only when he feels fresh again will he be able to tackle all the problems we face. He's probably having a lie-in because of his incredible age, so don't let us keep you from whatever squirrels do at this early time of morning. Rest assured, all problems will become clear as a bell when Old Elder brushes the sleep from his eyes and speaks.'

'Then I demand to speak to Sedge,' said the squirrel, stubbornly. 'I'm not sharing my problems with a magpie who talks too much. It's a listener I need.'

'How dare you!' said the magpie, shocked. 'I'll have you know I've appointed myself nautical pilot for this voyage. Anyway, Sedge and his family have gone for a swim and a watercress breakfast, if they can find one. I spotted their blunt noses gliding in convoy a minute or two ago.'

'Typical water-voles, always thinking of their bellies,' snapped the irritable Chief Squirrel, bounding back into the slim branches. He paused and issued a warning. 'Tell Old Elder I'll be back and with an even longer list of complaints. The more we squirrels are snubbed the more our problems will grow.'

Since the flood, other animals had stowed away in order to survive. Somewhere in a hastily enlarged knot-hole aboard the ark were two dormice, fast asleep. Long-time residents of the old oak, they had been snoring contentedly when the waters struck. Disturbed by the violence and noise, they had paddled sleepily across to the Great Bough and made themselves new rough-and-ready quarters, oblivious to the bustle of the Willow people, who were trying to save as many precious lives as possible.

The dormice had soon been snoring as peace-fully as before. It was said that dormice were the wisest folk in the world, that they knew the answers to all the questions ever asked. But what was the use of waking a dormouse to ask a question when the wise answer petered out into snores? The squirrels ignored dormice. The always-tired creatures could not be relied upon to attend a meeting and cast a vote. And a snore could not be counted as a legally raised paw no matter how wise that snore sounded . . .

Three badgers had also scrambled aboard to escape the waters. Soaked and shivering, the male badger described their shocking experience. 'We were bumbling about sniffing berries and talking to the trees as usual when we were swept off our paws by a wall of water,' he said, his eyes wide as he recounted. 'As we were being swept along, she of the lovely brown eyes began to have a nervous breakdown.'

'Your wife of the lovely brown eyes,' nodded the kind Willow people, 'who squats, trembling, beside you.'

'Then our son, who was floating beside us,

also began to behave in a strange way,' went on the badger, shaking his head in bewilderment. 'He has always been quiet and sensitive but suddenly his hazel eyes began to shoot sparks of rage.'

'It was the flood what done it,' said the young badger, his eyes wary and darting everywhere. 'One minute I was talking to the trees and the next I felt like a tearaway badger who needed to bite and destroy things. At this moment, if someone said to me, "Get off this ark," I'd probably fly into a terrible rage and damage everything and everyone who got in my way.'

'If my wife was refused refuge on this ark she would have a second nervous breakdown,' wept the badger, brokenly. 'And I would probably snap to pieces myself if our sick family were ordered to walk the plank back into the cruel waves.'

'There, there,' soothed the kind Willow folk. 'You and your family are welcome to stay aboard as long as you wish. Don't worry, your nervous problems and your refugee status will be sorted out as soon as Old Elder finds the time. Just settle down and try to sleep if you can.'

Hearing those words, the three badgers returned to being the gentle souls they were and fell fast asleep. Their story had been told in desperation, in order to stay aboard the ark. The shrewd Willow people were aware of this. But not one soul seeking safety that day and night was turned away, no matter what unlikely tale they told . . .

For other creatures, the ark was merely a landing and launching pad. There was much coming and going of bees and butterflies, black bats and moths, hooting and croaking things too.

The sun was high and hot when Old Elder appeared from below. He was flanked by Robin and Fern. The oldster sat down on the deck of the ark and gazed around at the view the early risers had seen some time before. Water everywhere, in every direction as far as the eye could see. Except for that green blur on the horizon that seemed to be getting nearer. At that moment, Sedge and his family climbed back on board, Sedge taking his place at the side of his friend. Everyone waited expectantly. They all believed that this was the perfect time for a speech from their leader, and they weren't disappointed.

'My friends, my children,' Old Elder began, 'we have survived a terrible night and for that we give thanks. Now we must survive whatever this new day may bring. The Great Bough, now our ark, has kept us safe from the waters. Now we must guide it towards a new future for us all. Towards a fresh and welcoming shore.'

'We're drifting towards a shore at this very moment, Old Elder,' said an early riser. 'But the magpie, who's been out scouting, says there's not an oak to be seen on that particular one.'

'Just puny poplar trees,' grimaced the bird. 'And thorny hedgerows packed with noisy finches and sparrows. We'd be twittered to death if we set up home in such an awful place.'

'Then we must seek another landfall, said Old

81

Elder, determined. 'We must hoist sail and voyage on until we find a place where oak trees grow a-plenty. Fern, hurry below and alert the weavers. Tell them their work could mean the saving of us all. This ark is our hope and must be made shipshape.'

His words were a bit too late. The green land was looming closer as the ark continued its aimless drifting. On deck the weavers urgently sewed and trimmed rough-and-ready sails to the few spindly branches but there was not a breath of wind to fill them. With a rasping sound of timber on coarse sand, the ark juddered to a stop. Shocked and afraid, the folk aboard the ark had more frights in store as their ship of hope wallowed and ground upon the sandy shore.

All at once a stone came hurtling from the land to strike the young tearaway badger smack on his sleepily whistling nose . . .

Many Humans had watched the building of the dam and the flooding of the valley with mixed feelings. Some agreed with the need for a new reservoir, but most protested against the destruction of the valley, the trees and the wildlife that lived there.

The planners had brushed aside such arguments. People needed water for their taps and swimming-pools and garden sprinklers, they said. And the huge new reservoir would be perfect for sailing and water-ski jumping. Hotels would be built with car-parks and fun-fairs: just think of the tourists their lake would attract! The planners weren't much bothered about the protesters: they had the money and the important backers to push through the project. So – out of the way, we have work to do, no business at all to you.

Among the Humans with mixed feelings were three children. They had risen early that morning to see the result of the spreading waters. On a new and higher shore, they marvelled at the changed landscape, once a surging boil of water, now a vast, flat calm. They felt pride that their dam-building parents and others could transform a whole part of the world so drastically. Yet they also felt regret as they gazed at the scattered tufts of green that once had been the proud canopies of trees, now choked and dying. The children stood in silence on the shore, each thinking their own thoughts. It was one of the boys who broke the spell . . .

'Hey, look!' he shouted, pointing. 'Isn't that the strangest thing?'

It was a tree bough stranded and rocking in the shallows, strange because its few sticking-up branches were festooned with not only dying leaves but what looked like crude sails. As they stared, the boy spoke again. The other boy and the girl looked sceptical.

'I tell you I saw something move,' insisted the boy, and he picked up and threw a large stone. He chose another and drew back his arm.

'Don't,' said his sister, sharply. 'It's probably a small creature trying to save itself from drowning. Don't add to its suffering.'

'If the water wasn't still rising we could wade out and rescue whatever it is,' said the friend.

'I'll just throw this last stone to see if it moves again,' said the boy, and he hurled it. Two seconds later he was hopping around nursing his ankle and groaning with pain. The girl and the friend hurried to see what was wrong. The boy's howls of anguish were brushed aside as they examined his ankle. To their astonishment, the girl pulled from his flesh a needle-sized sliver of wood, barbed and feathered like the tiniest of arrows. They gazed at it.

Though the morning was so calm a sudden gust of furious air whirled around their heads. A raucous screeching from above caused them to duck as the magpie dived out of the sun, its claws clutching at their hair, its cries filled with scolding. It buzzed them twice again before flapping off in the direction of the stranded log.

'That's also very strange,' said the puzzled girl, smoothing her hair. 'Why should that magpie choose to attack us like that?'

'This is even stranger,' said the friend, holding the sliver of wood close to his eyes.' It not only looks like a tiny arrow, it is one.'

'Or a thorn from a bush, more like,' said the boy, scornfully. 'The waters from the dam must have torn up thousands of hawthorn bushes.'

'No, he's right,' said the girl, peering. 'This has been carefully crafted. See the carved barb and the flights. It's an arrow, all right.'

'And it stung too,' said the boy, rubbing his ankle. He took the arrow to examine it for himself. His clumsy fingers caused it to shatter into fragments.

'There goes the evidence,' said the girl, angrily. 'All the skill that must have gone into making that beautiful, tiny thing. Now we've got nothing to show to prove our story.'

'My dad's got a rowing-boat,' said the friend, thoughtfully. 'And there's no doubt the arrow came from that log wedged on the sand. I think we should borrow the boat. It's on a wheeled trailer in Dad's garage. We could easily sneak it out and have a borrow of it. I don't think Dad would mind too much if he didn't find out. We could bring it back here and row it out to that mysterious log.'

'Or ship,' said the girl. 'Don't forget the sails. It can't be all in our minds because we can still see those tiny sails fluttering as if begging for winds to blow.'

'And I can still feel that arrow.' The boy winced. As if anybody cared . . .'

Just then a brisk wind began to blow, filling the ragged sails on the log. It heeled over and very slowly began to sail back out into the silver sea.

'We'd better be quick or we'll lose it,' said the boy, urgently. 'Are you sure we can borrow the rowing-boat?'

'No problem, let's go,' said the friend.

Soon the three were running the short distance to home, their thoughts filled with all kinds of wild imaginings, though never once dreaming of the tragedy and real-life wonder they had stumbled upon . . .

'Good shot, Robin!' cried Fern, rubbing the young badger's bruised nose. 'That'll teach those wicked Humans not to throw stones at tragic castaways.'

'Oh, just a lucky arrow,' said Robin, modestly. 'But it made the Humans run away – that's the main thing.'

'Not before I'd had a few sharp words to say,' said the magpie, gleefully. 'Not only will an ankle be stinging but also six Human ears.'

'That'll teach them to bait badgers,' said Fern, satisfied. 'Our badgers on board have suffered enough. We need to build them up fit and strong so that they can cope with other ordeals that might come their way'

'What ordeals?' said the young badger, his hazel eyes narrowing. 'What are you planning for me and my sick parents? If anyone attempts to throw us over the side of this ark, I'll have one of my tearaway moods and run amok, biting and snarling.'

'Don't be a silly young badger,' chided Fern.

'You and your parents are now part of our voyage and your health is safe with us. So mop your bruised runny nose and go and comfort your mother, who seems to be having another weeping fit.'

'Quiet! Look!' cried Old Elder, his prayers answered. 'The wind is rising and beginning to blow us away from this terrible shore. Let's hope our sails are strong enough to withstand the fiercest gusts. Let's hope they have strength enough to steer a course.'

'But a course to where, Old Elder?' said Sedge. 'Who knows where lies the ideal shore where oak trees grow as plentiful as weeds, where rippling blue streams dash into each other for lack of room to meander?'

'That's where I come in as Chief Scout,' said the magpie, proudly. 'I'll be flying regular missions to check out every horizon we spy. If I spot a bit of paradise I'll be the first to know, and the rest of you second.'

'Let's just pray that the small ones won't have to

sail the seas for ever,' said sad Grandma Willow, as she limped up on deck. 'We old ones will willingly end our days drifting the oceans of the world if our children can one day be steered safely into the harbour of a new life.'

'I echo the words of my wife,' said Old Elder. 'In the meantime, let's take every advantage of the rising wind. Ahoy, brave Sailors all, keep your sails trimmed to the weather and bear hard on the rudder.'

'Let's go sailing,' cried jubilant Sedge. 'Sailing together in a happy ship of friends. For what could be better?'

'Thank Heaven for good friends,' whispered Grandma Willow. 'And what do good friends need most after pulling together to save us all? What else but plenty of good hot stew, which I'll go and prepare.'

The shivering refugees were grateful for Granny Willow's good heart. In time, when their own hearts grew less cold, a vital bond would be forged – but not yet. Some, though, weren't in the least bit grateful for the kindness of the Willow Clan. Though still dripping wet and shivering, Deadeye and his rascally gang, after scoffing the offered food, had stolen away and found a quiet hideaway in the bowels of the ark. Here, they huddled to plot against the very folk who had saved their miserable lives. Deadeye had a cunning plan.

'We'll pretend to be changed characters.' He giggled. 'We'll bow and beg the forgiveness of the Willow Clan with sad smiles on our faces.'

'I've got it – like lull and smooth 'em over,' sniggered Hemlock. 'Then what, Dad?'

'While we're oozing goodness and smiles we'll be secretly making and storing weapons,' chuckled Deadeye. 'Then, when the moment is ripe, when we're good and ready, we'll leap on Old Elder and his saintly clan and destroy 'em.'

'What about that Robin?' asked Hemlock, nervously. 'He's a fierce fighter and his friends look tough, too.'

'Cocky Robin and his friends will be the first

to die,' snarled Deadeye. 'The rest we can swat like nuisance flies. To you, my son, will fall the honour of personally killing Posing Robin for the humiliation he heaped on you back at the old oak tree.'

Hemlock gulped hard and began to bite his nails.

'Who can I kill, Chief?' asked Toadflax, the dim one of the gang. He looked peeved. 'During all our raids on the Willow Clan I was only allowed to hold the tethers of our water-vole slaves while you all went to war. And I've had a great idea for a brilliant new weapon, which I intend to make. When it's carved and finished, I'd love to kill somebody with it.'

'Your chance will come,' snapped Deadeye, impatiently. 'There'll be lots of enemies to go round.'

'When all our enemies are dead, what then?' asked Toadflax, mystified. 'Will we just have a huge victory party and live happily ever after? It sounds a bit dull to me.'

'And you sound very dull to me,' said Deadeye, giving him a vicious whack around the ear. 'Afterwards, we take over this ark, you fool. Then we'll sail like pirates along the shores we find, looting and burning all oak trees as we go.'

'That's more like it,' beamed Toadflax. 'I can't wait to use my secret new weapon against everyone who doesn't belong to our gang.'

The hidden-away ruffians burst into muffled cheers. What a wonderful life Deadeye had planned for them! They couldn't wait to start. Some immediately began hunting for suitable bits of wood to carve into sharp daggers, swords and bows.

'Remember, this is our secret,' warned Deadeye. 'The Willow Clan must not suspect a thing. As for the smarming and the talking that's needed, I'll do that.'

'Because you're an expert at being smarmy,' nodded Toadflax. 'I wish I was as smarmy as you, Chief. I wish I could be half as treacherous as you.'

Seven

THE HUMAN PURSUIT

It was a bright though breezy midday when the three children launched the rowing-boat on to the ever-rising waters of the reservoir. Climbing aboard, they scanned for a sighting of the mysterious log that had excited their curiosity.

Then the girl saw it. Some distance away, where the water met the sky, it was sailing an erratic course as its sails seemed to fill, then flop. The winds of the early morning were dying. Soon the sailing craft was once again a log drifting round and round in aimless circles.

The boy and the friend bent to the oars and

began to pull, the girl in the bows yelling directions. Gazing through her borrowed binoculars she was enjoying herself very much as she issued commands.

'Pull to starboard – or is it port?' she ordered. 'No, straight on.'

'In other words, you've lost it,' said the boy, disgusted and panting over his shipped oars. 'You can't even keep track of a drifting log, and we certainly can't when our backs are turned to it.'

'The water keeps dancing up and down and the sun's in my eyes,' complained the girl. 'I'm not a hawk.'

'We should have brought night binoculars,' sighed the boy. 'By the time she sights the log again we'll be needing them.'

'If we can just get a little bit closer it'll do,' said the friend. 'I've brought my zoom-lens camera. If I can get the log in my view-finder at least we'll have some snaps as proof of what we saw. I mean, first we see a log with sails and moving things on board, then one of us is shot in the ankle by a real arrow as tiny as a needle. Then there was the peculiar behaviour of the magpie we all saw fly back to that log. Even famous scientists couldn't shrug all that off as nonsense.'

'I can see it again,' cried the girl. 'Row a bit to your left, then straight on into the sun.'

Grumbling, the boys obeyed. Pulling and panting away, they could only trust in the girl's sense of direction and seamanship.

After what seemd an age of sheer slavery the boys were ready to give up.

'It's hopeless and it'll be dark soon,' said the boy, angrily. 'We'll be in trouble if we don't get home soon. They'll have search parties out and everything.'

'Keep rowing!' shouted the girl, excitedly. 'It's no more than fifty metres away, I'd say. Get the zoom-lens ready for action, and you'll need the flash in this fading light.'

After a few more vigorous pulls on the oars, the friend stood up in the boat and aimed his camera. Staring through the magnifying eye-piece, he gasped. As clear as if it was no distance away wallowed the log that had intrigued them so. But it was the activity he could see aboard that had caused him to gasp in astonishment. He began to click and click and click, the blinding light from the flash making the others shield their eyes. Then he clicked some more to make sure.

'Did you get some good pictures?' asked the girl.

'I hope so,' said the friend, still in a daze. 'We'll know when we get back home and develop the film.'

'If we ever do get back home,' said the boy, worried now. 'The water in this reservoir hasn't stopped rising all day. For all we know, our home shore could be twice as far away by now. If we don't start rowing back we could end up drifting until we've got long white beards.'

'I'm just praying your camera was working properly,' said the girl, as the boys pulled as hard as they could for the distant shore. 'In fact, I'm hoping there was a film in it. And I'm also praying that the flash thing was made for that camera, because snaps can come out funny if the click and the flash don't work at the same time. Oh well, we can only keep our fingers crossed that we've captured some evidence on it.'

'Will you please shut up while I'm rowing?' said the friend. 'Just keep your fingers crossed that we manage to get back to shore. But just to put your mind at rest the camera's brand new, the flash worked perfectly and what I saw through the view-finder will make you sit up and pinch yourself.'

'Good, we'll develop the film first thing in the morning,' said the girl, happily. 'Our dad's got a little darkroom he's taught old Grumpy here to use.'

'Just guide the way to the shore,' snapped her brother. 'I'm starving for my tea.'

Eight

AN UNEASY TRUCE

Old Grandma Nightshade had barely recovered from the ordeal she and her clan had suffered, but that didn't stop her being up and about as soon as her ancient bones would allow. On rising her thoughts were of deep shame. Shame that down the years Deadeye and his cronies had heaped abuse and cruelty on the Willow Clan, only to be rescued by those kind people when in dire need.

Her next thoughts turned to practical and familiar matters. She felt an urgent need to prepare a large cauldron of hot broth for the shocked and shivering folk who crammed the meeting-hall. Yet she had neither a cauldron nor ingredients. Her intentions being good, her instinct was to steal to provide for the helpless ones.

Quietly she moved through the passages of the ark until she found herself in a large room that could only be an emergency kitchen. Upon the walls were hung cooking utensils and bunches of dried herbs. Peering around, Grandma Nightshade spied a large black cauldron that would suit her purpose perfectly. Glancing further, she noticed a fireplace and dragged the pot and the ingredients she needed close to it.

Suddenly, a soft voice sounded over her shoulder. 'Perhaps we can cook together, the pot is big enough,' said Grandma Willow. 'What with all the hungry mouths we have to feed, the task needs four willing hands. Though our clans are enemies, everyone is in need of nourishment after the ordeal we've endured.'

So began a firm understanding and friendship that would last through thick and thin. Both ladies were wise, and knew about good and evil. Both knew it was easier to love good people than evil ones. But the grandmas also knew that love was a strange and forgiving thing. While preparing the enormous stew, they agreed that everyone would be treated exactly the same, as far as filling bellies was concerned. Through the sorrows and the strife to come, they would never veer from that vow.

'On my knees, Old Elder,' wept Deadeye, tears running down his scarred cheeks, 'I thank you for saving the lives of my people. Can you ever forgive us for all the wrongs we've done you in the past?'

Grouped behind him, Hemlock and the ruffian gang also looked suitably sorry for their past misdeeds.

'They must think we're fools to believe that,' said Robin, his bow ready to hand, 'though one must admire Deadeye's acting skills.'

'And his tears are actually real,' said Fern, puzzled.

'Being familiar with watery things, I once heard a story about a crocodile,' said Sedge, interrupting. 'Crocodiles also weep in the hope that their victims will drop their guard. While the tears are warm, the heart is as cold as ice. Our Old Elder is too long in the tooth to be taken in by a crocodile sobbing on his knees before him.'

'The Willow Clan still feel anger for the past but they won't bear malice,' Old Elder was saying. 'Especially not for the young and the innocent members of your clan. We're willing to put all angers behind us if your clan will join with ours to help bring this ark into a safe harbour.'

'Thank you, Old Elder,' fawned Deadeye. 'We won't be found wanting. Just snap out your orders and we'll jump to obey them.'

'Old Elder,' protested Robin, 'Deadeye and his gang might look and sound sorry but how do we know they really are? They can't shrug off a lifetime of evil just like that.'

'Mention the crocodile,' whispered Sedge, in his ear.

'After all,' Robin went on, 'Deadeye and his mob might well be a swarm of crying crocodiles.'

'You mean bees,' giggled Meadowsweet. 'Bees swarm, crocodiles merely congregate. I know because I'm composing a poem called "Where the Bees Swarm There Swarm I, With a Stung Rose Do I Cry".'

'More Meadowsweet rubbish,' scoffed Teasel. 'Fancy crying because of a bee-stung rose.'

Fern shushed them as an argument began to flare.

'I'll take note of your concern, Robin,' said grave Old Elder. 'But it is my decision that, from now on, Deadeye and his friends will be judged by their future deeds. We'll need many strong and willing hands to continue and complete this voyage. If our old enemies work beside us for the common good, then so will they be judged.'

'You won't regret trusting us, Old Elder,' grovelled Deadeye. 'Our future deeds will make you gasp in astonishment. You watch and judge how quickly we change from our old ways.'

'And I'll be watching your new ways,' promised Robin. 'Be warned, if just one of your new ways threatens the safety of my friends and family then this bow of mine will settle the matter in a very old way.'

'We must have faith in our leader, Robin,' chided Fern, softly. 'He knows Deadeye well. He was never moved by those crocodile tears. Everything Old Elder does he does for a purpose, that purpose being the survival of the Willow Clan.'

'Now, let us make plans,' said Old Elder. 'First of all, the sick and hungry must be tended. And I mean the needy people of both clans. There will be no pinched cheeks and empty bellies aboard this ark. Who's in charge of the stores and the cooking?'

'The two grandmas,' answered Fern. 'At this moment, they're stirring and sweating over hot cauldrons without a shred of clan hatred between them. Can't you smell the delicious aroma drifting up from below deck?'

Old Elder smiled briefly. 'Now to our other tasks. This ark must be scrubbed and made ship-shape. The weavers must learn the tricks of the wind to make better sails, to turn those tricks and capture the winds fast. There's also the problem of the animals who scrambled aboard the ark to avoid the flood. They must also be attended to. In short, there are lots of jobs for us all to do.'

'How about an important job for Sedge?' shouted the young water-voles. 'The brave Sedge, who almost had his ear speared off by wicked Hemlock. Who valiantly ferried the expedition to the head of the valley and back again, without a murmur about his lumbago. Then what did faithful Sedge do? Faithful Sedge slipped quietly back into his home in the bank of the stream because he hates being praised. So why is Old Elder, our father's best friend, not heaping praise and important jobs on a water-vole bursting with merit?'

'How the young babble and boast!' said Sedge, embarrassed. 'If I did a good job then I want no reward.'

'Certainly I know you want no reward, old friend,' smiled Old Elder, 'but there is a vital job on this voyage that only you can do. To sail successfully, we need to know the depths and the shallows of the waters. We need to know the direction of the currents in order to steer the ark. We need to know where snagging obstacles are so that we can avoid them. In fact, we need an experienced pilot. What do you say, old friend?'

'The post of pilot doesn't sound very ringing,' said the stubborn young water-voles. 'We insist that our dad is called Supreme Chief Pilot, for he deserves it.'

'I'll gladly serve as pilot aboard this ark,' said Sedge, simply. 'And I'll treat every ripple as a tidal wave, such will be my devotion to duty.'

'Now to our magpie friend,' said Old Elder. 'Our voyage into the unknown will depend very much on him as time passes.'

'I know,' said the bird, delighted. 'For my eyes and my brain are vital for the mapping of the many shores we may encounter. And like Sedge, Old Elder, I desire no reward for my faithful service. Though if folk want to call me Supreme Chief Scout there's nothing I can do to stop them.'

'And I certainly won't stop them, dear friend,' smiled Old Elder. 'You're already familiar with your job, of course, to make regular flights ahead of the ark to search out the shore we seek.'

'As always, I'll be the keen eyes you can trust,' vowed the magpie. 'I'll be tireless in the service of this ark. In fact, I'll have another scout soon, you never know your luck,' and off he launched into the blue sky.

'Please, Old Elder,' begged Deadeye, cunningly. 'Give me and my people some honest work for our idle hands. We need to prove our total loyalty.'

'Very well,' said Old Elder, sternly. 'You can start by bailing out the water that's seeped into the galleries of the ark. Then you can scrub the deck. You can also fetch and carry for the people tending the distressed and needy.'

'Can't you find dirtier, harder work for us, Old Elder?' pleaded odious Hemlock. 'We so wish to make amends for all the pillaging we've done in the past. Bailing and fetching and carrying are jobs we'll come to love. We want horrible work we'll immediately hate.'

'I won't love bailing and scrubbing,' said Toad-flax, the dim one. 'I'd rather sharpen my sword and have a good scrap – ouch!'

'More of that talk and I'll box your other ear,' said Deadeye, angrily. He addressed Old Elder humbly. 'We'll begin our work at once. The ark will be as dry as a bone and the deck will be scrubbed till it shines before my gang and I are finished. And may I say, Old Elder, I'm quite overcome by the way we've been accepted into your clan. I think I'm going to weep again,' and he lurched away at the head of his gang to find buckets for bailing and brushes for scrubbing . . .

'More crocodile tears,' warned Sedge. 'Robin, my friend, you are wise to remain on guard while that treacherous bunch are aboard this ark.'

'I'll be awake while sleeping,' promised Robin. 'I'll never sleep with both eyes until that evil band depart to where they belong. To somewhere down below where it's very hot, I hope.'

'You are a worthy son of the Willow Clan, Robin Goodfellow,' said Sedge, his voice warm. 'Once you were youthfully cocky and brash but now I know your mettle. While innocents sleep under your protection, let the villains beware.'

'You're ignoring us, Robin,' complained Fern, tugging at his green sleeve. 'We have an awful lot of work to do and Old Elder can't organise everything.'

'There speaks *your* pilot, Robin,' grinned Sedge. 'As for *this* pilot, he feels the call of the sea; and the peace and freedom there.'

Soon all the able-bodied were busy making

the ark as shipshape as possible. The hardest workers were Deadeye and his gang. Throughout the day they bailed and scrubbed as if their lives depended on it. Some Willow Clan members working beside them felt their fears and suspicions beginning to wane. Perhaps the Nightshade gang really had changed for the better. Others weren't so sure. It was a huge leap from evil to saintliness in one go. Was it all a clever and cruel trick?

Yes, it was, for Deadeye had spelled out his plan in the hideaway early that morning. His vicious followers knew exactly what to do when the time was right and their Chief gave them the word. In the meantime, they would bow and scrape and work as hard as possible to mask their real, and wicked, intentions . . .

Robin and Fern and their friends went along with the unlikely change in their enemies. Old Elder had urged them to, though he knew himself that a truce based on hatred and lies wouldn't last. But the oldster was prepared to pretend that peace was in place to gain time in these anxious days. There were so many innocents aboard the ark, both Willow and Nightshade. His mission was to protect them all. He had confided his thoughts to Robin and Fern, who had reluctantly agreed to go along with his wishes. But they and their friends kept their weapons close by, and watched and listened for the first sign of trouble from their Nightshade foes.

The new day was filled with autumn sun and stillness. The weavers had worked through the night to stitch bigger sails to catch more wind. These were bent on to the limbs of the ark to the loud protests of the squirrels. Yet what use were sails with no breeze to fill them? Until the weather turned and a brisk wind rose, the People and their friends would be going nowhere, though many were glad of the lull, for this snatch of calm in their voyage. Still recovering from the flood ordeal, few cared if the ark drifted in circles a while longer. How nice it felt not to be dashed about by the wind and weather.

Others were as busy as ever. The magpie flew in from another scouting mission. Clasped in his claw was a shiny toy from a cereal packet, but that was his own private business. Old Elder and Robin looked up expectantly as the bird perched on a twig above their heads.

'No sign of our dream shore, I'm afraid,' he said. 'Just miles of stubble wheat-fields and fences. Not an oak tree to be seen. But cheer up, the world is full of horizons waiting to be discovered. I'm bound to spy the perfect one as we sail along.'

'That's the problem,' said worried Old Elder. 'We've new sails but no wind to fill them. Which means we're using our precious stores while going nowhere. I'm beginning to doubt my decisions as leader.'

'I don't doubt them,' said Robin, stoutly. 'We might be adrift on this endless sea but it's better than lying crushed and drowned among the splinters of our old tree.'

'I don't need to tell you about faith, old friend,' said the bird, gently. 'Faith in yourself and the faith of others who cling to your words. We'll find that horizon one day, never fear. Now, excuse me while I nip home for a rest, only it was sweltering hot out on that false horizon.'

For a while Old Elder and Robin were left alone with their thoughts which, though unspoken, were filled with dismay as they gazed at the mirror-like glinting waters that stretched in every direction. They also turned to watch the figures moving around the deck engaged in their tasks. One figure suddenly straightened and approached.

'Excuse me, Old Elder,' said Deadeye, sidling up. 'My friends and I would also be grateful for a rest. We've been hard at it for hours, bailing out and scrubbing everything in sight.'

'Yes, you well deserve a break,' agreed Old Elder. 'Go below and get some food, and I'm pleased to see you fitting in so well as members of the crew.'

'Dare I tell you, leader?' fawned Deadeye. 'But in the early hours of the morning I came on deck and looked up at the stars and a wonderful feeling of peace swept over me. It was as if all the wicked things I'd done during my life were suddenly forgiven. My friends and I really love bailing and scrubbing for it seems to wash away all one's sins. But at the moment we're completely worn out. So, if you'll pardon us, we'll go for your generous snack and a short nap.'

'Don't nap too long, Deadeye,' said Robin, eyeing him. 'We wouldn't want you to go back to your old idle ways, now, would we?'

'Oh, don't worry about us ever being idle again,' said Deadeye, returning his gaze.

Looking into the other's good eye, Robin felt as if his blood had turned to ice. Hate and rage and a deep longing for terrible revenge seemed to shine from that evil, unblinking orb.

Very softly, Deadeye said, 'Oh, proud Robin, have I got busy work to do when I find the right time for it . . .'

Hiding their smirks, Deadeye and his gang slunk below and grabbed some food, before hurrying through the bowels of the ark to their small dark hideaway. They were soon working hard at what they did best: carving weapons, amid curses, and aching for the time when they could cast aside their cloaks of peace and rampage about as in the good old days.

Hemlock brandished a spear he had made, a murderous gleam in his eyes. 'This is for the heart of that strutting Robin,' he snarled. 'And how I'll smile when I send it winging home.'

'And this,' spat Deadeye, holding up a knobbly club, 'is to bash out the brains of that preaching Old Elder.'

'And this,' said dim Toadflax, holding up a shapeless lump of wood, 'is to destroy all the rest of 'em . . . when I've finished it.'

'But it's just a piece of wood,' said the others, puzzled.

'It won't be when I've finished it,' gloated Toadflax. 'It's my brilliant new weapon I told you about. When it's carved I'm going to fit a springy bit on the side for extra power. The problem is, I don't know which side to fit it to.'

'Why don't you fit it on your thick head?' jeered Hemlock.

'It wouldn't work,' said Toadflax, shaking his head. 'It has to fit on to the side of my secret weapon to work properly.'

'Oh, shut up, Toadflax,' groaned the gang. 'Why can't you whittle a sharp dagger or a sword like everyone else? Inventing secret weapons needs brains, and you've got none!'

'Before we return to bailing and scrubbing slavery, we'll sing our war song to keep our anger bright,' said Deadeye.

Softly, for fear of being overheard, the gang began to chant,

'Let us carve hate in the weapons we love,
Thorn-pointed, every tip hardened in fire,
Mutter dark threats against those who dare cross us
And lust for the battle that's coming . . .'

After some more evil doings in the gloomy hide-away, the gang went back to the kitchen, where they gobbled down second helpings of stew, served by the kind and sweating grannies. Then they trooped back on deck, pictures of humbleness as they resumed their hated work.

As always they were closely watched by Robin and his friends, whose hands never strayed far from the weapons they carried. They were not impressed by Deadeye's avowed change of heart. They remained alert for the merest sign that their enemies were about to launch some treachery that might take them by surprise.

Old Elder was still sitting, gazing out over the water, pondering the many problems he faced. Beside him slumped Sedge, his whiskered nose in his paws, fondly watching his family frolicking in the water below, though part of his mind worried about Old Elder and the burdens he carried. The gentle water-vole felt so helpless. He voiced his frustration. 'If our ark has circled in the same spot once, it's circled a hundred times,' he said, angrily. 'Will the wind never do its business?'

'And we with dwindling stores and so many

innocent mouths to feed,' said the impatient leader.

'Of course, we could always adjust our passenger list,' said Sedge, grinning. 'For a start we could throw Deadeye and his mob overboard. That would ease the food crisis. And what a cheering set of splashes they would make.'

'You, of all folk, should know the law of the sea,' replied Old Elder, though he smiled as he said it. 'The law states that rescuers must treat those they save from the water as they would their own family. So, having saved many lives from the flood we're now responsible for the well-being of them, no matter who they are, no matter how much we might detest them personally.'

'I'm relieved you smile as you say those solemn words,' said Sedge, grinning ever wider. 'It's good that your wisdom is tempered with humour.'

'Though a cheering set of splashes I'd enjoy to hear,' chuckled the oldster. 'A wonderfully tempting thought . . .'

'Just winging in with my latest report,' gasped the Chief Scout, out on his claws with fatigue as he perched on a twig above. 'Nothing interesting land-wise, I'm afraid, but weather-wise we're in for a spell of luck. During my flight to the south I spied great banks of cloud heading this way. Knowing the sky and its moods I can say with confidence that quite soon the winds will whip up and we'll be in for a good blow. So, my friends, prepare for some exciting sailing before this day is out.'

'Robin . . . Fern . . .,' called Old Elder urgently. The two came running. 'Tell the weavers to strengthen the sails to withstand a strong buffeting. Warn everyone below to prepare for more tossing about as we get under way. Assure them that it's all to the good, for at last we'll be sailing again. Sailing ever closer towards the shore of the new and peaceful valley we yearn for. Urge them to keep their spirits high and sing, for happiness always comes at a price . . .'

His messages were quickly conveyed around

the ark. While the weavers and the deck-crew busied themselves with hauling on ropes and stitching slippery sails, from below came the strains of song. At first there was little enthusiasm as the people in their misery tried to sing. Then, surprisingly, Teasel, Meadowsweet's hateful tease, stepped forward and recited to the fearful crush a poem he had thought up on the spur of the desperate moment. It was such a singalong poem that Meadowsweet forgot she detested him and began to hum along. Teasel's words and her tune blended so beautifully that soon all of the People were singing along at the top of their lungs. It was a song of hope and defiance. It was a song that would go down in the histories of the People for future generations to recite, to hum as they imagined those terrible times at sea aboard the sacred ark. It seemed as if every soul bound on the quest joined in, to roar the new song that united them. To the stamping of a hundred feet it drowned out the ominous howl of the rising wind . . .

'Buffet cruel winds
At the Ark of the People
Lash us with stinging white spray,
Frown angry clouds
On the Ark of the People,
Your terrors will fade as shines our new day . . .'

'There are some who've got nothing to sing about,' shouted the Chief Squirrel, swarming down through the sails to put a damper on the mood. 'We squirrels want to know why we're living in misery while you lot can sing below? Do you realise each time you fiddle with the sails you damage our homes? Some of us have even been tipped out of bed because of all your hauling on ropes. Why have sails at all? Have you never heard of peaceful paddles? I demand an immediate Grand Meeting to thrash out why we squirrels are being treated as second-class passengers. And don't think we've forgotten Fern's swimming-pool insult that is still to be settled. There is also the press-ganging question. We

122

want to know why we squirrels are forced to be sailors when we hate the sea and its choppy waves. We think it's certain to be against the law. Have you decided we don't count, Old Elder, once my dearest friend? I must warn you that when the vote is taken at the next Grand Meeting you'll be swept from power if you don't show more kindness. By the way, are there any nuts knocking about down here, only we've run clean out up top . . . ?'

'A supply of nuts from the stores will be sent aloft,' promised Old Elder. He appealed to the angry squirrel. 'Trust me a little longer, my friend. We still face many dangers on the journey we've undertaken. Please understand that the sails are being readied to take advantage of a great gusting wind that's heading our way. Tell your family to take heart that soon we'll all be living happily in a new oak in a new valley. Then when we are settled we'll hold all the meetings you wish.'

'I'll keep you to that,' said the squirrel, sourly. He turned to scurry back into the flurry of flapping sails, tossing a word of warning over his shoulder. 'And I'd advise you to deliver the supply of nuts immediately . . . unless you want a squirrel mutiny on your hands . . .'

'No sooner said than done,' called a relieved Old Elder after him, issuing the necessary intructions to a fuming Fern . . .

Deadeye was scrubbing nearby and listening. He edged nearer until he was almost scrubbing the deck around Old Elder's feet. His gang also began to close in, their ears straining to pick up the conversation.

'Excuse me, Old Elder,' said Deadeye, 'did I hear some mention of black clouds and gales on the way? My friends and I would like to volunteer our services, should the ark be in danger. Perhaps me and my honest band of sailors could tug ropes and swarm aloft and batten down hatches and things. For we've developed warm feelings for this ark and its crowded masses. It's almost like home to us now. Perhaps me and my jolly tars could take over the policing of the ark in case there's another terrible storm and the People start to run amok. We'd be very good at putting down riots – in a kind way, of course.'

'With the minimum of force and weapons,' said Hemlock, getting his father's drift. 'We'd bring quiet and order in no time at all.'

'Remember the Nightshade gang is still on trial,' cried Fern, hotly. 'After a bit of phoney bowing and scraping, bailing and scrubbing, do you really think we would trust you with authority and weapons?'

'We hold the weapons on board this ark,' said Robin, outstaring Hemlock's murderous gaze. 'And in our hands they'll stay, as long as I have breath in my body. I resent that you should dare to address Old Elder as if he were a fool or born yesterday.'

'Nevertheless, they can be of help,' said Old Elder. 'Deadeye and his friends can stand to and help Sedge spot dangerous rocks and snags, should the gales blow into a storm and our scout

125

magpie is unable to take off to warn of perils ahead.'

'I'll be no good at spotting snags,' said Toadflax, at his stupid best. 'At the moment I'm puzzling over a snag that's hit the wonder weapon I'm carving in secret. Every time I try to fit the springy bit it's always in the wrong place. Maybe I need two springy bits.'

'What wonder weapon?' said Robin, his eyes wary, his bow flexed.

'Don't be alarmed, fearless Robin,' smirked Deadeye. He tapped and shook his head, then rolled his bloodshot eye. 'Our Toadflax enjoys to make toys. Just harmless, childish toys. I'm surprised our lovable idiot should alarm you so, courageous Robin.'

'Alarm me?' said Robin, annoyed. He looked just a bit shame-faced as he retorted, 'It's just that I never drop my guard and never will while the smell of enemies lingers aboard this ark.'

'But you'll drop that guard one day,' growled Hemlock, beneath his breath. 'And when you do I'll drop you with a single thrust from my spear.'

Hemlock's words were just a petulant mumble to the listening ears but there was no mistaking the stark threat in his eyes as he and Robin faced each other, clear in their understanding that there was no room in this world for both . . .

Then it was back to business for a brisk and hopefully long, storm-free sail that might cast them upon an ideal shore, where they could start their lives anew.

Nine

THE SEA SO WIDE AND WE SO SMALL

Early that morning the boy had developed his friend's photographs. What he saw shocked and astounded him. Seeing the prints, the girl went wild with delight. They dashed with them, still limp and damp, across to their friend's house where he was soon poring through them, an expression of satisfaction on his face.

His view through the eyepiece had not deceived him after all. The evidence was clear and in full colour. He went and found a magnifying-glass and returned.

'It was a badger you saw moving on the log and threw a stone at,' he gasped. 'But what can these scurrying creatures be? And they *were* sails we saw. See the small people – yes, people. But look for yourselves.'

'It's impossible,' cried the girl, gazing. 'They're really people just like us but tiny, titchy small!'

The boy pushed her aside and seized the magnifying-glass. He sighed in wonderment. The mini-people were dressed in greens and browns, and seemed to carrying old-fashioned weapons.

'The thorn in my ankle,' he shouted. 'It really was an arrow!'

'Fired in revenge for the stone you threw,' said the girl, pleased. 'It serves you right and I hope it still stings.'

'So, what do we do now?' asked the boy. 'Handled right, these snaps could make us a fortune. Like selling them to a newspaper.'

'No, we keep them secret for a while,' said the friend. 'You know how silly adults can be. Look at the fuss they make when they see a comet in the sky – the end of the world is upon us and all that. If they saw our photographs, the reservoir would be filled with boats crammed with newsmen and tourists from around the world, clicking cameras and frightening the tiny people we've discovered.'

'I want to make an important point,' said the girl. 'The little people we saw on that sailing log weren't doing it for a publicity stunt, hence the angry arrow in my brother's ankle. I believe the flooding of the valley is to blame. I think the people on board that log are trying to sail it away from the fury of the rising waters, which means they're bound on their voyage in order to survive. Which also probably means they could use some help. I suggest we make another trip in the rowing-boat, but this time loaded with supplies like baked beans or something in case they're starving on that log.'

'Would such tiny old-fashioned people like baked beans?' asked the boy, doubtfully.

'Everyone, young or old, loves baked beans, silly,' scoffed his sister. 'It's turnips and cabbage everybody hates.'

'With the water still rising, that log could be far away by now,' warned the friend. 'It could mean a much longer trip this time. If we go we'd need to leave notes for our parents saying that we'll be late for tea because we're playing a ping-pong knockout match in the school hall.'

'So long as we don't hint where we've really gone,' said the girl, quickly. 'Because that secret must be kept from the world.'

'So, it's back to the oars,' said the eager friend. 'Lucky we didn't take the boat home. Lucky we left it tied to a tree above the water-line. Let's hope the flood hasn't risen much higher.'

'Can't I just hint to the newspapers about our astonishing photos?' asked the boy, hopefully. 'Just a small interview. Then we'll be famous all over the world. On telly – on the Internet even!'

'No, it's our secret,' said the girl. 'Many small lives could be hanging in the balance out there on the water. We don't want the place swarming with nosy telly people. Your dream of fame will just have to wait.'

It was past midday when the three arrived back at the shore. To their annoyance, the boat was slopping with water and had to be bailed out, losing them precious time. At last they climbed aboard and launched out on to the calm, sunlit waters. Compass in hand and binoculars slung around her neck, the girl took up her position as captain in the bows. The others leaned forward over their oars and began to pull.

'This heat is ridiculous,' grumbled the boy, sweat pouring off him after less than a hundred strokes. 'You'd expect it in the Sahara Desert but not here in the middle of England.'

'Autumn heatwaves are always the worst,' agreed his panting friend.

'Don't fuss about being hot, just row for the north,' shouted the girl, consulting her compass.

'If we knew where the north was,' snapped the boy. 'We've discussed this before. How can we see where we're going with our backs turned? It's obvious we can only see where we've come from. It's all right for you playing Captain Bligh in the bows, but we have to do the rowing!'

'I think I can see something,' cried the girl. 'It looks like a little black dot against the sky but it's bound to be the strange log. Pull straight on, but try to bear to your left, if you can.'

'I've had it,' said her brother, collapsing over his oars.

'And me,' wheezed his friend.

'But the log is in our sights now,' beseeched the girl. She rummaged among the supplies. 'Here, drink this can of Coke between you, then get back to work. Another couple of hundred strokes and we'll be nudging alongside our prize.'

'Aye, aye, sir,' muttered the boy. He turned to his friend. 'She practises all this discipline on her hamsters at home.'

'We can take it,' grinned the friend. He drained

the Coke can and took up his oars again. 'Come on, only a few hundred more punishing strokes to pull.'

'Now I can see the log sharp and clear,' yelled the girl, peering through her binoculars. 'And – would you believe? – our quarry is sporting extra and bigger sails! I can't see any movement, though.'

'I should think not,' gasped the boy. 'Only fools like us would slave in this stifling heat.'

'The small people are probably resting in the shade of the sails waiting for the wind to blow,' said the girl.

'And they're about to get their wish,' said the friend, nodding at the black clouds building up. 'Autumn heatwaves are often followed by heavy autumn storms. And, if I'm not mistaken, here comes one now.'

'The winds are certainly springing up,' agreed the boy, turning his hot face to the cooling breeze. 'I think we should abandon this trip and get back to shore before the weather breaks.'

'But we're so near,' pleaded the girl. 'And I had so many plans!'

And she had. She had glanced at her watch and was shocked to see it was almost five o'clock. So much to do and so little time to do it, she worried. And would the storm hold off long enough?

She had brought along a small tape-recorder. With it she planned to interview the tiny people. She had so many important questions to ask them. Like, how did it feel to be so incredibly small, and what did they think about the state of the world? She was also keen to hear their views on fashion, for surely just green and brown could become very boring? Then there was the photo-opportunity she had planned. While she was relaxing and chatting with the small people, her friend would be taking as many snaps as possible. She believed the recordings and the photos would be the astonishing proof that would launch her career into television and then Hollywood film-making. Now it seemed that all her hopes and dreams were about to fall apart.

your feet,' shouted the friend. 'It's got a long rope and should be strong enough to hold us. But you'll have to do the grappling because we need to row as close to the log as possible.'

Streaming with rain and buffeted by the fierce wind, the girl stood bravely in the bows directing them, a coil of rope in one arm, the sharp anchor in her free hand. As the short distance between the boat and the log finally closed, she spun and tossed the anchor at the stern of the bucking log. Her aim was true and only just in time. The anchor bit and held its grip on the waterlogged wood. Then, suddenly, the wind turned, the sails snapped and billowed, and the log and the rowing-boat were racing through the white-capped swells.

Bruised, exhausted and sopping wet, the three slumped into the bottom of the boat in a tangle of oars and bits of rope and fishing tackle. It seemed not to matter now, for the strong pull of the log's billowing sails was deciding their direction as the anchor and the strong line held.

And all of a sudden a comforting feeling came over them. It was impossible to describe. They no longer felt the fear of being in a small rowing-boat in a vast, wild sea. They felt cradled and safe, the boat no longer dangerously open but strangely enclosing. The threatening sky above had receded, as if being viewed through the wrong end of the girl's binoculars.

The eerie feeling increased as they were pulled along behind the now strongly sailing log. They felt no fear at all, in spite of their life-threatening situation. They felt they could trustingly surrender their will to survive to another, stronger will. As the storm continued to rage, they snuggled together in the bottom of the boat, sharing each other's warmth as they fell fast asleep.

It was as if that physical contact had magically soothed away their terrors. The act of throwing the anchor to link the two vessels had mysteriously bridged a huge gap between two very different worlds. Worlds that had never met, except through myth and legend. The girl's lucky throw had united the People and the Humans for the first time in their long histories, for good or ill.

Who could say how two ways of life could come to terms in calamitous times like these, if at all? Putting their trust in whichever fates guided them the three children slept through the roller-coasting storm, and in their innocence, could not see tomorrow and what it might bring.

In its own time the storm abated, the winds dying and the black clouds drifting away. Suddenly the night was filled with a blaze of stars, as if the violent hours had never been. The moon rode in confidence again, casting reflecting yellow light on to the gently flapping sails of the ark, and into the trailing rowing-boat where three children slept. And beautiful peace and silence reigned over the calming waters.

Ten

RESCUE AND HOT STEW

Morning came with the waters as still and as sunlit as they had been on the morning before. Waking, the children rubbed their eyes, and sleepily tried to come to terms with their situation as their memories of yesterday returned starkly to mind. It was clear that the boat and their bodies had taken a battering, hence the leaking planks and their bruises.

The friend made the first positive move. Rising painfully to his feet, he attempted to peer over the side of the boat to see where they were. To his bewilderment, he found that the once low sides of the boat were so high as to be impossible to climb. The planked sides once lapped over by water now reared as high as the walls of a prison. He fell back, exhausted, the boy and the girl rushing to free him from the heap of soft material that had broken his fall – the bed they had slept in last night.

Confused, they stared up at the climb that had defeated him. Surely this was not the small rowing-boat they knew so well? But, yes, it was, even down to the baked bean tins they had taken aboard. As proof, to their horror, a can of Coke rolled lazily towards them. What had once been small enough to slip into the pocket of a jacket was easily twice the size of any one of them. Bewildered and looking further around the floor of the boat, they noticed that they were sitting on a huge pile of clothing.

'That's my T-shirt,' said the shocked girl, pointing. 'I can tell by the tomato-ketchup stain down the front.'

'And those are my trainers,' whispered the friend. 'The exact worn heels. My mum always moaned that I scuffed along when I walked.'

'And my jeans,' said the boy, amazed, fingering the frayed blue trousers. 'My mum said yesterday I was growing out of them, but I don't think I have. Those jeans were made for a giant.'

It was then that the frightened three stared at each other to discover they shared their nakedness, their skin white and shrivelled by torrential rain. Then a voice called. The startled children looked up to see a boy peering down. He had toffee-coloured eyes and wore a jaunty feathered cap. Peering down beside him was a girl with a snub nose, eyes the colour of honey, who was wearing a russet-hued dress and a hat with purple daisies round the brim.

'We're Robin and Fern of the Willow Clan, and

we see you're in need of rescuing,' said the boy. 'We're throwing down a rope. Grip it tight and we'll haul you to safety. Then we'll take you aboard our ark, for the Willow Clan always helps folk of the People in distress.'

'What clan do you belong to?' called Fern, as she and Robin lowered the rope. 'You three look nothing like any clan I've ever seen before.'

'Let's leave the questions for the moment,' Robin said. 'Let's get them out of there and into some dry clothes.'

After much effort the three children were hauled from the depths of the boat. Shivering with cold they stood in the prow of their once small boat that had taken on enormous proportions from their suddenly tiny point of view. Their shaking eased as the welcome sun warmed their bodies after those long hours of damp darkness below. Though apprehensive about the bewildering events that had swept them up, all three felt safe in the care of the two strange children, who had briskly taken over their lives.

The boy Robin quickly explained how they were to be transferred to the log that rolled beneath sagging sails a little way off. He pointed to the sagging anchor-line that spanned the two vessels. 'Fern and I balanced across,' he said. 'We'll go back the same way. It's a bit scary but not too bad when you get used to the sway. I'll go first, you three will follow in the middle while Fern brings up the rear. We'll all hold hands tightly – and remember not to look down in case the shimmer on the water makes you feel dizzy. Just trust us and we'll soon have you safe and sound.'

Clasping hands the five carefully inched across the anchor-line, pausing now and then to adjust their balance against the swing. After the frightening tightrope journey they at last stood on the slippery bark deck of the ark. The children had no time to gaze around before they were quickly ushered below to be fitted out in green and brown tunics and hose. Then they were bustled into a hollowed-out cavern that served as a kitchen, where two kind old ladies filled wooden bowls with delicious hot stew. Gratefully and hungrily the children gulped it down.

'Excuse me for being nosy but I'll ask you again,' said Fern. She was looking curiously at the girl's bright yellow hair. 'What clan do you belong to? Why is your hair so fair and your eyes so blue? The People most usually have brown hair and eyes, so our history books say.'

'Whereabouts in the old valley did you live?' questioned Robin. 'Was your oak destroyed in the flood like ours? You're certainly not of the Willow or Nightshade Clans. How did you come by such a strange-looking vessel? What happened to the rest of your clan?'

'We don't have clans, we have families,' explained the girl. 'We live in houses far away on the shore. As for oak trees, we have one in our garden. It was still standing when we left to come on this trip. As for Fern's questions about my hair and my eyes, well, we Humans are very different in that way. Some have got black hair and black eyes, some have got red hair and green eyes, but we're all Humans just the same.'

'Humans?' gasped Fern, her eyes wide in horror. 'The terrible enemies we've always been warned to hide from? The giants who drove us to live in the trees to protect our way of life?'

'Hardly giants now,' said the boy, ruefully. 'We've shrunk out of our clothes to become as tiny as you. How, I don't know, but I'm fed up already. If you've cast a spell on us then you'd better uncast it. I'd like to know what was in that stew, which was the best I've ever tasted. More spells, I suppose. So when do we turn into statues or frogs or something?'

'We've rescued Humans?' said Robin, angrily. 'I've a good mind to throw you all over the side this minute. It was because of you that our valley and our homes were destroyed. It's because of your meddling with nature that we're adrift on this sea in search of a new and peaceful land.'

'Please,' implored the friend, trying to calm things down. 'We're sorry for the things we

146

Humans have done to the world. But all Humans don't think the same. We certainly don't. We were sad to see the valley destroyed to make a reservoir. It was when we came down to the water's edge that we realised the wicked thing our fathers and mothers had done in the name of progress. It was when we saw this log in distress that we felt truly sad and determined to help.'

'But then my stupid brother threw a stone,' said the girl, shame-faced.

'And received an arrow in his ankle for his pains,' nodded the friend. 'And well deserved, as he knows himself.'

'It was only a titchy arrow,' said the boy, scornfully. 'It only stung a bit.'

'An arrow like this one?' smiled Robin, drawing a slim shaft from his quiver. 'A good shot, then, wouldn't you say?'

'Only perfect, Robin,' said Fern, adoringly.

'Perfectly placed and richly deserved,' said the girl, sincerely. 'Now we're at your mercy and also in your debt for rescuing us. But please don't throw us over the side because we're Humans and because of my brother's attitude. Although he's very childish at times, he's only Human, after all. We'll gladly make amends for all the wrongs our race has done to you,' and she began to weep into her empty stew bowl.

'Those aren't crocodile tears,' said Robin, quite moved. 'So, Fern, what shall we advise Old Elder to do with these Human children?'

'I'll shoulder the blame for all the Humans in the world,' said the boy, bravely. 'Because you Willow people probably hate me the most, I'm willing to sacrifice myself if you'll spare my sister and friend. My last request is that you turn me into a frog before you chuck me over the side of your ark. Then I'll have a fair chance to breast-stroke to the safety of the shore.'

'Again you speak of spells and magic,' said Fern, puzzled. 'Why do you think we possess such powers? We're just ordinary members of the People and the Willow Clan going about our simple lives and trying to make them better. Why do you believe we could turn you into a frog, silly boy?'

'Because I've read books and seen pictures of you lot, that's why,' said the boy, stubbornly. 'You may live in oak trees instead of under toadstools but you all have blobby noses and wear caps with feathers in. I've read all about how you stir bats' wings and cuckoo-spit into delicious stews to make children dizzy. Then you offer them three wishes if they get the answers right to three riddles, but they never get the answers right because there are no answers to the riddles in the first place. Anyway, I'm not in the mood for meaningless riddling. So just turn me into a frog and I'll take my chances in the water – for I'll never bow and scrape to goblins who cheat, even if you did rescue us from our leaky boat and give us some trendy clothes to wear.'

'I've never heard so much nonsense,' said Robin, annoyed. 'Your history books must be a pack of lies if they teach you such things. We of the People get by with good common sense not magic.'

'If there's no magic involved then how have we grown so small?' said the girl. 'Can you answer that, for I'm very worried about it?'

'I can only answer with good common sense,' replied Robin. 'Everyone who lives in the world of the People is small. So it stands to reason that if giant Humans come barging uninvited into our world they must also be small. How do you think you three fitted in? If you were still giants, Fern and I couldn't have saved your lives. In other words, common sense made you small.'

'Small is always better,' added Fern. 'That's also common sense.'

The three strange-looking newcomers from the sea had attracted a small crowd of interested youngsters.

'Magic or not, I still can't understand it,' persisted the boy. 'How come my mum always said

I was gangly then suddenly I'm a little titch? At least I'm still the tallest one here.'

'Put that boast to the test,' challenged Teasel. 'Stand back to back with me and we'll see who's the taller. Even before I prove it I know I'll tower above you, just as I tower above everyone else.'

'I've got the angry feeling that Teasel is going to win this contest,' sighed little Meadowsweet. 'Just as he always wins the poetry contests, with his bad rhymes about ducks gobbling down innocent girls.'

The boy and Teasel stood back to back, straining on their toes to be taller. To the disgust of his opponent and Meadowsweet, Teasel won by a fraction. In fact, no more than the thickness of an oak leaf.

'Enough of these games,' said Robin, sharply. 'Shake hands on a truce and no more quarrelling. We have serious business to discuss with Old Elder. Namely, what to do with these shrunken Humans in our midst. Bring them along.'

Teasel and the boy sportingly shook hands before Teasel took the boy into custody as his prisoner, soon to face the wise judgement of Old Elder. The girl and the friend were also taken under guard. The girl was guarded by Meadowsweet, who chose to link arms in a friendly way with the captive, who had such lovely corn hair and cornflower blue eyes.

'Do you realise?' whispered Foxglove, to no one in particular, her eyes shining with excitement. 'This is the second truce we've had in two days and we've barely begun our sailing nightmare. The first truce with the wicked Nightshade gang, now this one with the Human children, who are wearing our clothes and enjoying our stew as if they had a perfect right – as if our ark belonged to them. When will all these truces end, I wonder? I hope we don't have another one tomorrow, because truces are only good for postponing problems. And how can we sail in search of our new valley in harmony, with heaps of problems piling up?'

'Old Elder is good at untangling truces,' said Coltsfoot, firmly. 'He may be a bit doddery on his feet, but his wisdom never stumbles.'

Meanwhile, the fearful three were being escorted on to the deck of the ark to have their fate decided by the leader of the Willow Clan. Would he be sympathetic and understand, or would he order them to be thrown over the side of the ark to sink or swim?

Eleven

JUDGEMENT AND SENTENCE

'So, you admit to being Humans,' said Old Elder, gravely, addressing the three children standing before him. 'You also confess to chasing our ark and throwing a grappling anchor aboard. Why, if not to spy on us? A further charge against you is the serious one of impersonation. Do you deny that by using some cunning Human magic you have shrunk yourselves from giant to normal size to pass as members of the People? For our history books tell us that all Humans are huge, clumsy creatures, who stride through the world crushing everything under their clumping feet.'

'We don't know why we're suddenly so small, Old Elder,' said the confused girl. 'We thought you might tell us. As for being giants, only my brother was rather tall for his age. Our friend and I always thought ourselves quite normal in height. But it isn't fair to accuse us of being spies just because we've lost a lot of weight. We surely don't deserve to be thrown overboard just because we're a lot shorter than we used to be.'

'As Chief Scout, I wish to bear witness against these three,' said the magpie, perched above. He narrowed his keen eyes. 'Gazing at their faces I can definitely say that these are the culprits who threw the stone from the shore while our ark was wallowing on the rocks.'

'A cruel stone that hit me on the nose,' shouted the young badger, 'causing severe bruising, and causing my mum to have another nervous break-down. If we badgers are picked on for much longer I'm going to run amok, not caring what damage I do in my fury.'

Foxglove and Coltsfoot hurried across to pat and soothe the small badger and his mother, tenderly wiping away their tears with the sleeves of their tunics. Then they hurried back to the crush to listen agog to more unfolding evidence in the trial aboard the ark.

'Old Elder,' the friend was imploring, 'let me explain the whole story and prove we aren't the sneaky spies you think we are.'

And with the suspicious eyes of the Willow Clan fixed upon him, he told how, when the dam was opened to flood the valley, he and the others had raced through the meadows to watch the waters rise. He spoke about the strange log they had noticed, wallowing in the tide, which appeared to have crude sails fluttering from its branches. Then they had noticed signs of life aboard. It was then that the boy had thrown the stone, something he bitterly regretted. In fact he was so sorry that he had been pleased to receive a sharp arrow in his ankle as punishment. Yes, he went on, they did recognise the Chief Scout of the ark as the magpie who had angrily buzzed their heads, and rightly so. He told the fascinated crowd about the rowing-boat trip, and how the three had been determined to help the survivors on the log.

He went on to describe the second trip of the previous day and the desperate chase across the water, then the girl's heroic throwing of the anchor in order to save their souls as the storm blew up. His now sympathetic audience listened raptly as he described the wild and black night as they were hurled about and screamed at by the pitiless winds, a night when everything became topsy-turvy then dreamlike and calm. The next thing they clearly remembered was waking to find themselves incredibly small, then being res- cued from their boat by brave Robin and Fern, to whom they would be forever grateful. And now here they were, he finished, a boy and a girl and a friend throwing themselves on the mercy of the Willow Clan.

Immediately, the sad and heroic story was greeted with storms of applause by the sympathetic Willow Clan. They, too, had suffered through the terrible storm, and it was pleasing to know that these Human children had set out in their boat to offer help to their clan in peril on the sea. It was also reassuring to note that when Humans were cut down to the correct size there was little harm in them at all.

'I think I speak for most of us when I say the friend's story sounds absolutely truthful to me,' said Fern, dabbing at her honey-coloured eyes.

'The tale was told too honestly to be lies,' agreed Robin. 'I think that while the boy Human did and said some silly things, their hearts were in the right place. But it's up to Old Elder to decide their fate, he being our wise and ever-right leader.'

The three children stood close together, their hands linked. They trembled as the gaze of Old

Elder seemed to pierce into their souls. But they remained brave, for they had told no lies and had no secrets that Old Elder could unmask.

They had a sudden ally in the leader's oldest friend. 'Drowning is a cold and lonely death, Old Elder,' said Sedge, edging to squat close. 'I'm not a jury but I also think the Human children are innocent and no threat to us. If they are convicted and thrown overboard, my family and I will dive after them and ferry them back to safety, such is my belief in them. But I'm wasting my words, for you and I are always of a mind.'

Old Elder smiled, and was just about to deliver his verdict when there came the sound of hurrying, stamping feet. On to the deck burst some of Robin's band, anger on their faces.

'Old Elder, Robin,' gasped their spokesman, 'we were patrolling as ordered and we discovered a small hideaway deep in the bowels of the ark. Here in my hands is the evidence of some of the things we found in that place. In my left hand I brandish a wickedly carved spear with the words,

"My home is the heart of Robin," etched along its shaft. In my right hand I hold a strange lump of wood with a springy bit stuck on the side – some secret weapon, no doubt. Old Elder, I regret to say that some folk aboard this ark have set up a hidden weapons factory, and we all know who they are.'

The gathered Willow Clan gasped in outrage and horror. After generously rescuing the Nightshade gang from the flood, their kindness had been thrown back in their faces. For the secret weapons factory was the type of business venture in which only Deadeye and his evil mobsters would engage. Deadeye, who was sweeping the deck nearby, hurried to protest his innocence, his sole eye welling tears.

'On my honour, Old Elder,' he whined, 'my friends and I know nothing about the mass production of weapons. How many leaves must we turn over to be accepted as honourable members of this ark? With deep regret, I voice my suspicions about who is really responsible for the

the spokesman mentioned,' said Toadflax, in all his glorious dimness. 'I haven't finished it yet. I'm still pondering whether to fix the springy bit on the other side to increase the power. Ouch!'

Deadeye and Hemlock had moved in quickly to stifle his outburst with vicious punches to his ribs, but too late.

'Condemned from the mouth of a fool,' said Old Elder. He turned his angry gaze on cowering Deadeye. 'You were given the chance to make good but, alas, goodness is not in you. I gave you the benefit of the doubt and now I'm taking it back. Prepare to be fairly punished.'

'Throw the evil lot over the side of the ark,' yelled some of the Willow Clan. 'This voyage will be the safer for it. Let the sucking worms enjoy them, for they make our bellies churn.'

'How about if we scrubbed and swept and bailed twice as hard?' pleaded desperate Deadeye. 'If we slaved twice as hard we might become twice as good as we tried to be before. Throwing us over the side for the worms to munch would make you a murderer, Old Elder, and your heart is too soft to bear that terrible tag.'

'Anyway, there's no point in throwing me over the side because I can't swim,' said Toadflax, the logic of that quite clear in his simple mind. He turned to Deadeye and sighed. 'This is another mess you've got me into.'

'A long imprisonment will be the punishment,' said Old Elder, his judgement made. 'Deadeye and his gang will languish in jail until this voyage is safely over. Robin, march the rascals away and see they don't escape.'

'March them away to where, Old Elder?' said Robin, puzzled. 'There's no jail on the ark – certainly no place secure enough to hold such desperadoes.'

'I see such a place,' cried the magpie, from his high vantage point. He flapped a wing and pointed with his beak. 'There, floating behind our ark. The boat of the Human children. A perfect prison, surrounded by water and easy for me to keep a scouting eye on.'

'Well thought, dear friend,' said Old Elder, pleased. 'Robin, do your duty.'

'I don't like the idea of that,' protested the boy. 'All our things are in that boat. We don't want those ruffians rummaging through them.'

'Some of the things aboard are rather personal,' agreed the girl.

'And it is my dad's boat,' insisted the friend. 'I think you should ask my permission before using it as a jail.'

'Be quiet,' hissed Fern. 'Don't get on the wrong side of Old Elder. Remember, you three haven't won your case yet. You still risk being thrown overboard.'

Snarling and vowing a terrible revenge, Dead-eye, his cursing son and their gang were hustled to the stern of the ark by Robin's stout followers. The Willow Clan, their animal friends and the children watched as the wicked plotters were forced along the anchor-line, yelling in fear as it swayed beneath their weight. Once aboard the rowing-boat they were lowered on ropes into the dingy depths to begin their sentences. Their echoing threats and oaths drifting up were terrible to hear.

'Be grateful that you'll be fed regular bowls of the grannies' stew,' yelled Robin downwards. 'Which is more than the Willow Clan could expect from you!'

'Expect much more from us, Robin Smugface,' hissed Deadeye, like a trapped viper, from the depths. 'For when we escape, as escape we will, your death and many others will be certain. As certain as, when comes the day you find your beautiful shore, we, the Nightshade gang, will rule it over your dead bodies.'

'Over *your* dead body in particular, Robin Prettyface,' screamed Hemlock. 'For I'll never rest until I spear you dead!'

'You should have chucked us over the side,' warned Toadflax. 'Because, looking around down here, I can see lots of useful bits and pieces I can make into an even more secret and deadly weapon – Ouch! Ouch!'

Robin and his friend turned away from the

sounds of Deadeye and Hemlock taking out their frustration on hapless Toadflax. They balanced swiftly along the line back to the ark. They were just in time to hear the verdict being delivered on the Human children.

'I've listened to your amazing story with great interest,' said Old Elder, rubbing his chin. 'But one thing puzzles me. Why didn't you save yourselves from the storm-lashed boat with the mighty powers we know you Humans possess?'

'Because we haven't got any powers,' shouted the boy, his short temper flaring again. 'We're just ordinary schoolchildren, supposed to be on holiday. If we had magic powers we'd have passed our exams with top marks. Anyway, if I had powers I wouldn't allow myself to be shrunk as small as this. Who wants to be this size when being tall is the aim?'

'We of the Willow Clan rejoice in our size,' said Teasel, indignantly. 'Especially me, I being taller than anyone else, including you.'

'Yet my brother is speaking the truth, Old

Elder,' pleaded the girl. 'We're just innocent children caught up in your quest to find a new oak tree in a lovely valley where you can build your lives anew. But please consider our lives. We didn't sneakily plot to board the ark. We just wanted to help. Then the storm blew up and caused all the trouble.'

'Now we're here we'd like to help in any way we can,' said the friend, sincerely. 'You rescued us, now we'd like to repay your kindness. And we share something in common, Old Elder. We three are also adrift and yearning for a welcoming shore. I miss the green, green grass of my front garden very much. So we'd be much obliged if we could sail on as friends as we search for our different shores.'

'Then, when we get to ours, Old Elder might turn us back to our proper size,' said the boy, butting in. 'I'm fed up being this tiny. I want to be gawky again.'

'Silence,' called Sedge. 'Old Elder is rubbing his brow again, which means he's coming to another wise decision.'

'The Human children will not be thrown overboard,' said Old Elder, breaking the breathless hush. 'I've decided to opt between kindness and caution. They will become members of our crew until they find the shore they also yearn for. They will be treated well, but their freedom must be restricted. When they move about the ark, an escort must be with them at all times. We can't afford to trust them completely just yet.'

'In other words, we're also being jailed but without walls,' stormed the boy. 'I demand to be chained hand and foot. Even that's better than being followed around by snoopers. Then, when my chance comes, I'll snap my chains and escape. Show me a prison and I'll show you the freedom tunnel I intend to dig.'

'Don't be silly,' said his sister. 'There's no soil beneath the ark. You'd tunnel straight into the water where the worms would be waiting for you.'

'You'll be held in the kindest custody,' Old Elder assured him, 'hopefully for not too long.

You must understand that, as leader of the Willow Clan, I must make sure you pose no threat to the success of this voyage.'

'We understand, Old Elder,' said the girl, her eyes watering with gratitude. 'We'll be loyal members of your crew.'

'Brown eyes or blue,' murmured Fern. 'Both colours are true.'

'Fern should stick with being a leader and leave the poems to me,' said little Meadowsweet, annoyed.

Teasel, starding nearby, couldn't resist a dig. He cleared his throat and said, solemnly, 'A typical Meadowsweet poem by Teasel the famous bard.

"Then Old Elder he did spake
And Meadowsweet did umbrage take,
That Fern should dare, a poem make . . ."'

'Oh, do shut up, for goodness sake,' cried Meadowsweet, angrily stamping her foot. 'I wish Old

Elder had banished you to prison along with the Nightshade gang, but without bowls of the grannies' stew.'

'I'd welcome the experience,' baited Teasel. 'All great poets need to suffer. I'd probably write poems of genius behind prison walls. The starvation and the despair would bring out my best rhymes.'

'No arguing among you young ones,' ordered Old Elder. 'We have serious matters to discuss. Chief Scout?'

'Yes, Old Elder,' said the magpie, smartly.

'Fly high and wide, and hopefully bring us news of a steady breeze,' said the oldster, his hands clasped in hope. 'A breeze strong enough to fill our sails, to push us on our way again.'

'I won't return without one,' vowed the bird, taking off in a flurry of black and white feathers. Soaring upwards he shouted, 'Look to your laurels, O weather! I'll have a balmy breeze or bust!'

'Right,' said Old Elder, looking happier. 'We've solved the problem of the Nightshade gang, we've sorted out the status of the Human children. Now all we need is for our magpie to rustle up a brisk breeze.'

'And he will, I'm sure,' said Fern, also looking cheerful. 'If there's a breeze about, he'll scout it out.'

'May I make a request, Old Elder?' asked Foxglove, shyly. 'After all the worries of the day, can we laugh and joke and play again?'

'And give ourselves three hearty cheers?' asked Coltsfoot.

'Why not?' smiled Old Elder. 'Why not indeed?'

And to express their relief the clan, their friends and the children gave three mighty cheers that shivered the timbers of the ark – to the intense anger of two stowaways. To everyone's astonishment, two whiskered noses popped from a knot-hole in the bark. 'Some folk are trying to sleep,' complained the first dormouse. 'The raging of the storm was sent from Heaven so we had to put up with that. But there was no divine reason for all that cheering!'

'Which came straight from Hell to our sensitive ears,' winced the second furry dormouse. 'Don't you clan people ever sleep?'

'We're very sorry,' said Old Elder, trying to hide his grin. 'Would you two care for a drop of hot stew? You must be hungry after tiring days of sleeping round the clock.'

'No, thank you,' was the prim reply. 'We have a few nuts to nibble if we wake up feeling peckish. Just peace and quiet, that's all we ask,' and down they popped again.

'I heard that,' yelled the Chief Squirrel, swarming down from above. 'Dormice pinching our nuts, indeed! I must warn you, Old Elder, my family are seething with revolt up there. Their mutter is that they aren't being listened to. Every time the sails fill with wind they're bounced out of bed. They won't stand for much more of having their complaints brushed aside. They're demanding to know why it's taking so long to

172

reach this new valley of milk and honey and nuts. I must warn you again, Old Elder, the mood is getting ugly up there.'

'All our troubles will soon be over, Chief Squirrel,' said Old Elder soothingly. 'We are certain that a breeze will soon spring up to sail us to the shore we all so long for.'

'Breeze equalling more flapping sails, I suppose,' grimaced the squirrel. 'Very well, Old Elder, but I can't contain the anger of our squirrel youth much longer. The last thing we need is a revolution. And tell those thieving dormice to leave our nuts alone!' With that, he raced back into the curtain of sails.

'A breeze! A breeze! And wafting close on my tail feathers!' cried the Chief Scout, gliding in.

'Robin, Fern, crew, stand by to make sail,' ordered Old Elder. 'And may the next lap of this voyage be our last.'

'The sooner for my family and I to be gliding in a cold stream through a lovely valley,' said Sedge, his soft eyes glowing, 'with tall leafy oaks for the

People to hack with their axes. Not like vandals, of course, but to make homes fit for heroes.'

And the blessed breeze continued to blow, filling the sails of the ark to send it scudding across the seemingly endless sea.

Twelve

A COMING TOGETHER

As the ark sailed on, to nowhere in particular, Old Elder turned his attention to the Nightshade Clan survivors below deck. Before he went down he gave instructions to the sailors and the children remaining above, first to the children. 'Remember to keep a sharp look-out for any attempt to escape from the prison-boat,' he warned. 'We know the wiles and cunning of Deadeye and his bunch very well by now.'

'Aye, aye, Old Elder,' chorused the girl, the boy and the friend, pleased to be given such a trusted and important task.

'Sedge, the team manning the tiller will be banking on you to shout out if a rock or a floating danger imperils our smooth sailing.'

'My eyes are searching like gimlets as you speak,' yelled the water-vole, clinging to the gently tossing bow.

'And our ears are finely tuned to hear his cries of "Danger ahead",' shouted the volunteer tiller crew. Foxglove and Coltsfoot had never felt so grown-up and trusted in their lives as they clung grimly to the large, bucking piece of wood that served as a tiller. 'Don't worry, Old Elder, we'll steer this ark into the jaws of Hell if you command us to, for we're simple Jack Tars in love with our wise captain.'

'Chief Scout,' said Old Elder, raising his eyes to the magpie's favoured perching twig. 'Are you attending to your important duties?'

'No need to say, Old Elder,' replied the bird. 'The whole of the world lies stripped naked beneath my beady gaze. Nothing escapes my eyes, not even my own comings and goings.'

Satisfied, Old Elder, flanked by Robin and Fern and others, went below.

The scene in the gloomy gallery was pitiful to behold. The young and the old of the Nightshade Clan lay listlessly around, their misery plain. They knew their lives were in the hands of the Willow Clan, the folk their leaders had waged war upon for as long as could be remembered. Yet even in despair their hope refused to die. Hadn't the Willow Clan snatched and saved them from the flood? Hadn't they provided dry clothing and hot stew, plus acorn bread to mop it up? So would this kindness and mercy continue? They knew that Deadeye and his hated gang would have shown no mercy if the situation had been reversed. So the survivors of the Nightshade Clan could only huddle close to each other and pray that their saviours were not playing a cruel trick to make them suffer more.

Then, as if rehearsed, two persons rose from the crush to confront Old Elder and his followers as they entered the gallery. Weaponless, they didn't flinch as their new masters approached. They were Pimpernel and Pansy, the young hope of the Nightshade Clan. Forced by circumstance to lead, they felt afraid, but that was nothing new. Having lived under the tyranny of Deadeye and his despised gang, they knew what fear meant. Yet still they had risen. And having found the courage to do so they stood their ground, determined to defend with their lives the many innocents now in their charge.

'Who are you?' asked Old Elder, not unkindly. He reached to restrain Robin, who had bustled forward.

'My name is Pimpernel,' said the rusty-haired boy, proudly. 'And I have words to say. On behalf of the Nightshade Clan, I thank you for rescuing many of us from the flood. We are now your grateful prisoners. We heard the loud voices up above sentencing Deadeye and his gang to prison and we're not sorry, for we hated them too. But if you've come for more revenge against our clan I offer myself as a sole sacrifice. Heap your hate on me, hack me down, but leave my people be.'

He was briskly moved aside by the girl. She had tumbling, raven-black hair and eyes as black as glowing grapes. Her skin was as pale as snow, highlighted by pink spots on her cheeks. Her quick temper was evident as she spoke. 'My name is Pansy Nightshade,' she said, her snub nose proudly high. 'As the daughter of Deadeye and the sister of Hemlock, I demand that you take your pound of flesh from me. Though my father and brother are deservedly in jail I'm still of their blood, as Pimpernel is not, so I'll take all the blame for the evils done in the name of our clan. Just leave our innocents alone. Harm one hair of their heads and I'll claw like a demon until you in turn beg for mercy.'

'I was supposed to deliver the defiant speech,' said Pimpernel, crossly. 'Your job was to back me up.'

'I'm sorry I stole your thunder,' said Pansy, patting his shoulder, 'but your speech needed pepping up with a bit of fire and my temper got the better of me as usual. With apologies I pass the defiance back to you.'

'So, triumphant Willow Clan,' said Pimpernel, bravely, 'take no notice of Pansy and take your revenge on me. Here I stand and here I'll stay until you strike me down. But don't delay my end, for my dear mother is watching and weeping.'

'We have no desire to avenge ourselves on you or anyone,' said Old Elder, shaking his head. 'The evil ones are in jail. You and fiery Pansy and all of your clan are welcome guests aboard this ark, and you'll be treated the same as we treat our own. In the meantime, is there anything we can do to make your people more comfortable?'

'Yes, there is,' piped a voice from the crowd. A tiny lad rose and approached Old Elder. In his hands he bore his licked-clean stew bowl. 'Please, Old Elder, I want some more, and another hunk of acorn bread to mop it up.'

'And what's your name, little hungry one?' smiled the oldster.

'Nettles,' was the prompt reply. 'Because I can be very irritating at times.'

'More you shall have,' said Old Elder, his eyes twinkling. 'Take yourself and your ravenous friends off to the kitchen and appeal to the grannies in charge.'

Thus the ice was broken and relieved laughter rippled among the people of the Nightshade Clan, who had been fearing the worst. Fern was pleased to see these miserable people relax at last. Though she wasn't pleased to notice Robin gazing at Pansy with a silly grin on his face. Pansy, dressed in hand-me-downs from the ark's stores, hardly looked the height of fashion, and her long, thick eyelashes and jet-black eyes were more startling than pretty. Anyway, in Fern's opinion, real heroines had more to do than stand around looking striking while there were so many wrongs to be righted in the world. Tossing her mousy hair she turned to listen to the serious talk going on between Old Elder and Pimpernel. Proud, though gaunt and tousled, Pimpernel certainly radiated a rugged charm, Fern thought . . .

'On behalf of my clan, I thank you,' Pimpernel was saying. 'Your trust and your hospitality will not be abused. As you say, we all belong to the People, whether we are good or bad. So what are your plans for the future? For we are eager to help.'

'The plan is sketchy but our hope is strong,' Old Elder replied. 'We intend to sail this ark across the sea until it comes to rest on the ideal shore where the new valley of our dreams will be waiting for us. Now that our enemies are safely in jail we can proceed on our voyage in peace.'

'All the rotten eggs in one basket,' explained

Fern, proudly. 'One of the typical wisdoms my grandfather always thinks up. He'll fill a whole chapter of our history books when his time comes to stop breathing. That's how respected he is. Even the Human children aboard our ark are in awe of him.'

'Human children?' cried Pansy, turning round, a look of terror on her face. 'On this very ark? And you condemned my father and brother for being wicked! Who are more evil than the Humans we've hidden from since time began?'

'I'll explain everything to Pansy,' said Robin, drawing the distressed girl aside. 'I'll make her see that her fears are unfounded.'

'I bet you will,' snapped Fern. 'And while you're mopping her lustrous eyes and encouraging her toothy grin, remember the dangers we still face in the middle of this sea with our ark heading nowhere in particular!'

Meanwhile, Pimpernel was about to address the huddled masses of his clan. He was urged gently forward by Old Elder.

'My dear family and friends,' he cried, in ringing tones. 'At last our days of fear are over. Deadeye and his cronies have been clapped into jail and will bully us no more. Long may they languish there!'

Cheering and foot-stamping greeted his words. Holding up his hand for silence, he continued with more good news. 'Since the dam burst and the storms broke, we've lived in a nightmare of worry and uncertainty. We couldn't understand why the Willow Clan would rescue and feed and clothe us, when they'd suffered so much at the hands of our wicked leaders. Why should they show mercy? we asked. The answer is simple, my friends. Kindness and forgiveness, that's what they found in their hearts. Now the Willow Clan have invited us to take part in a great adventure. Aboard this ark, and under the leadership of Old Elder, we are sailing in search of a paradise valley where we can live in peace and plenty for ever more.'

'We're not deserving, but we welcome it,' cried

a joyous voice, above the renewed clapping and stomping.

'I now call upon Old Elder to speak more,' said Pimpernel. 'And you'll notice he doesn't bawl and threaten like Deadeye did, for he's gentle and caring in word and mood. Listen closely to the hope and security he offers us.'

'Hope and security! Such gifts to treasure,' sobbed a lady with nine small ones and a husband in jail with Deadeye.

'People of the Nightshade Clan,' said Old Elder, solemnly, 'the voyage we are bound on may be long and arduous with many dangers along the way. I warn you, the land we seek may only exist in hopeful dreams. We have been driven from our ancient valley. Who can say if another waits for us?'

'I'm certain of it,' cried Pansy. 'Our paradise lost will lead to our paradise regained, with all the beauty of the old, but without the ugliness.'

'But back to the voyage,' said Old Elder, briskly. 'We'll need lots more strong arms on deck to keep the ark sailing and shipshape. There's also lots of work to do here below. So let's join together and strive to find that shore where the oak trees grow tall, and where crystal-clear streams gurgle over pebbles between green-rushed banks. I'm certain we'll overcome the obstacles and reach our goal. We have courage and determination enough, for we are the People.'

'We are the People,' chanted the happy throng. 'We are the People,' they sang, dancing in celebration of their new-found confidence and their freedom from the brutal rule of Deadeye and his gang.

'And now, People of the ark,' smiled Old Elder, 'are there any questions?'

'Yes, quite many,' said a voice.

Silence fell over the Nightshade Clan as a scarred youth limped forward, a wary look on his face. His name was Quickthorn, and he was much respected among his clan for bravery and bluntness. Though young, he had always stood up to sneering Deadeye, to ask questions the evil tyrant couldn't answer. Each time he had been told to shut up and had been severely beaten for his impudence. Also he had been thrashed often for daring to compose and read aloud beautiful poetry, for Deadeye hated art and self-expression. Quickthorn wore his scars and his badly twisted ears like badges to be proud of as he addressed Old Elder.

Among the agog listeners were Meadowsweet and Teasel, who had dashed down from the deck to check out the rhyming style of this acclaimed genius of the Nightshade Clan.

'Can I ask any questions I wish?' said Quickthorn. 'Will you twist my ears if I ask one you don't like?'

'Your ears are safe with me,' Old Elder assured him. 'Fire away without fear, young Quickthorn.'

'Where is this new and beautiful valley?' asked Quickthorn, bluntly.

'I don't know,' Old Elder admitted.

'So, can I take it that this ark is sailing aimlessly to nowhere in particular?'

'Not quite,' replied Old Elder, frowning slightly. 'I'm sure we're sailing in the general direction of our new home.'

'In the hope that the ark will bump into it?' probed Quickthorn. 'Because that's how it sounds to me.'

'It's all to do with navigation and keen scouting and things,' said Old Elder, a bit irritated now.

'And if we do find this valley at the end of some rainbow, how do we know it will be thick with towering oak trees and tinkling streams?'

'Because the People wish it to be so,' replied Old Elder, angrily. 'If we can't dream and strive to replace what we've lost, there's no point in living at all.'

'Now do I get my ears twisted?' asked Quickthorn. 'Because you're going red in the face, which in always a warning sign when my questions are becoming hard to answer. Though, I must admit, Deadeye lost his temper much quicker than you. He would have flown into a right old rage by now.'

'I'd sooner twist my own ear,' said Old Elder, ashamed of his outburst. 'Please forgive me, small Quickthorn.'

'I will, and gladly,' said the lad, smiling for the first time. 'I have two more questions that involve my personal happiness. May I ask them?'

'I'll be really annoyed if you don't.' Old Elder grinned.

'May I play an active role in this voyage to this maybe, or maybe not, valley that exists more in dreams than reality?'

'We wouldn't sail another mythical wave without you,' said Old Elder, amused. 'I intend to make the most of your talents, cynical little poet!'

'And now my last and most important question,' said Quickthorn, suddenly looking very eager and anxious. 'Will I be allowed to wear an outfit exactly like Robin's, with a jaunty feather in my cap?'

'I'll measure you up myself,' Old Elder said, laughing. Then he sobered and spoke to the expectant gathering. 'But for now, please, no more questions. There's lots of work to be done, so let's get to it.'

The People began to disperse, filled with excitement and purpose. At last they had a dream to aim for that didn't involve the angry clashing of weapons and weeping. Their hopes were high as they set to work with a will, to make Old Elder's dream a reality for everyone.

'I can't imagine where Quickthorn studied poetry,' said disappointed Meadowsweet to her friends. 'All those questions and not one rhyme among them. Perhaps he could do with some of my rhyming coaching.'

'I could do with some coaching,' grinned Teasel, butting in. 'Would you know of a word that rhymes with nightingale because no-one on earth has yet thought of one.'

'Will you please leave me alone?' howled Meadowsweet, stamping her foot and storming off.

Back on deck again, Old Elder began to organise his extra crew and set them to useful work. Sedge, who had been peering over the side of the ark watching for rocks and hidden snags, declared that he hadn't spied a single one. His youngsters, who were proudly learning the skill, said neither had they, even with their eyes fully peeled. Foxglove and Coltsfoot, who were swinging happily on the tiller, agreed that the steering was as smooth as silk. It was the children at the stern of the ark who rushed to Old Elder with disturbing news, which was echoed by the Chief Scout magpie.

'Deadeye and his gang are brimming out of the bilges of the prison-boat,' gasped the girl.

'Like poison bubbling over the sides of a pot,' said the boy, with relish.

'I'm worried about the things we left in the boat,' said the friend. 'In clever hands some of them could be dangerous. I'm thinking in particular about Dad's emergency locker in the bows. I know he kept all his fishing stuff there. Lots of sharp hooks and things.'

'Deadeye and his gang wouldn't know how to use them,' scoffed the boy. 'They'd need to be Human and modern to figure out how they worked.'

'Didn't Toadflax hint that he was building a secret weapon?' said the friend. still worried.

'Toadflax is dim and thick,' laughed the boy. 'You heard him.'

'Many a genius was jeered at,' said the friend, 'before going on to astound the world with great inventions.'

'Pardon me, but Old Elder is present,' interrupted Robin. 'If you have worries you should tell him, not discuss them among yourselves.'

'My, just listen to the cursing coming from the prison-boat,' said the perched magpie, shocked. 'Enough to blister the ears of clean-living folk. And just look at the rascals, Old Elder!'

Everyone crowded to look at the boat trailing along behind the ark. Deadeye, Hemlock and a few others had somehow clawed upwards from the depths and were standing on the bows, shaking their fists and yelling vengeance against the Willow Clan and everyone who sided with them.

Deadeye and Hemlock even adopted diving poses as if threatening to swim back to the ark and slake their fury in blood. But they didn't, because they were cowards and afraid of getting their toes wet or, worse, of drowning.

'We've nothing to fear from them yet,' Old Elder comforted the frightened ones. 'Let them yell and shake their fists all they want. With the water between us there's nothing that wicked gang can do, for the moment. If the time ever comes when we have to confront them again, we'll be ready.'

'They certainly won't risk the balancing act along the rope,' grinned Robin. 'They were gibbering with terror before we'd got them half-way across.'

'I still say we should have made them walk the plank,' cried a stubborn lone voice. 'They should have been splashed overboard for the worms to feast on. I believe this clan is storing up trouble for itself with that wicked mob still alive and able to shake their fists at us.'

'I'm surprised the Human children haven't

been thrown over the side,' said Pansy, glaring at the girl's hair, which shone like gold in the sun. 'And blue eyes are a sure sign of cunning. Honesty has only ever shone out through jet-black eyes or sometimes brown, that's a fact in all of our history books.'

'I will not tolerate discord on this ark,' thundered Old Elder. 'The Humans have been judged as fit crew members.'

'And don't forget it,' shouted the defiant boy, at angry Pansy. 'Anyway, you can talk! Your father and your brother are convicted criminals.'

'Enough,' ordered Old Elder. 'All of us must learn to live together if we're ever going to reach our journey's end. I demand peace on this ark. We are now sailing steadily with all hands bent to their tasks. Mr Navigator, Sedge, is there anything I've forgotten to say?'

'Yes, old friend, there is,' said Sedge, gently. 'You've forgotten to admit you're dead tired. You're not getting any younger, you know. I suggest you have a nice lie down.'

'Perhaps you're right,' said Old Elder, who felt completely drained. 'But be sure to wake me if anything urgent crops up.'

'I will,' promised Sedge.

With the cooling breeze and the warmth of the setting sun on his face, the old leader fell fast asleep. His rest was deep and secure in the knowledge that the ark on which they depended was in safe hands. With sails billowing, and glowing red from the setting sun, the ark sailed serenely on.

As the ark of the People ploughed through the sea in search of a dream, a boy in a small round coracle-boat paddled the waves in the opposite direction in search of his own. His quest was to find the source of the River of Dreams, the sacred flow that had moulded the lives of his clan since the first pages of their histories had been written.

After two days of wearying paddling, the boy was ready to give up. According to the history books, this sea should not exist. He was paddling to nowhere on something that should not be here. Bewildered and exhausted, he curled into a ball in the bottom of his coracle and fell asleep . . .

He was woken by the warmth of the morning sun and the sound of a huge black and white bird screeching in his ear. After circling a few times, the bird departed. Rising shakily, the boy gazed around the endless sea. Fear returned as he noticed a sailing vessel heading his way. Could it be the Humans, and what would they do if he fell into their hands? All his life he had heard about the cruelties of which the giants were capable. Then, as the craft neared, he saw it was a huge log wearing hastily fashioned sails. Very close now, he could make out the scurrying figures aboard the log looking, thankfully, much like himself. Standing tall in his rocking coracle, he waved his arms and hailed.

Thirteen

A FISHER BOY CALLED FINN

Finn of the Fisher Clan had always yearned to be an explorer of places he knew nothing about. Ever since his father had failed to return from his voyage to find the source of the River of Dreams, the son was determined to follow in his wake. But this time the explorer would return in triumph. Unlike his worshipped father, he would not vanish without trace in the wondrous places he was eager to discover. Which was why Finn prepared so carefully.

In the bottom of his new-made coracle he stored rations of dried fish and freshwater shrimps in case the fishing was poor during his voyage. He also carried a spare paddle and extra clothing, plus a small mast and sail to hoist if the waves became rough and made paddling difficult. Not least Finn had made himself some smoked, fish-scale goggles to protect his eyes when he needed to gaze at the sun to get his bearings. For the Fisher Clan were sensitive to glaring light after living for so long in the gloom. Earlier, he had consulted the clan history books to learn all he could about the source of the River of Dreams. Alone in the small cavern that housed the precious parchments, he read aloud the few known facts.

'It is written that the River of Dreams began its journey from a spring on a hill in a far and distant land. From the hill it trickled down to be joined by other springs to become a stream. The stream began to flow through a great valley where it was widened by other streams to become a deep river. At the end of the valley it turned to flow through a gorge that made it froth and boil in fury before it dived underground. Once beneath the earth, it calmed to become the River of Dreams the Fisher Clan came to know so well. The existence of the Fisher Clan has always depended on their river that brings them fish to net and spear, and other good things to eat. It is said that the River of Dreams and the bounty it bears was sent as a kindness and mercy by One who refused to desert the People in their time of flight from the Humans . . . Thus was it written in those earlier times.'

'It's very little to go on,' mused Finn to himself. It was true. The scant information in the histories was hardly the detailed map all explorers needed to go forth and come back in safety. He stroked the ancient pages and imagined the fingers of his lost father doing the same as he, too, prepared to set off in search of the source of the River of Dreams. How sad that his father had only found

This was the Great Grotto, their sacred meeting place. From the inky darkness of the cave system came flowing the River of Dreams, sweeping majestically before their eyes before continuing its journey to another world beyond their understanding. The Fisher Clan always flocked to the Great Grotto when their hearts were in need of uplifting, and when their fish stocks were getting low. These gatherings were times of great joy for the clan, who spent most of their lives scurrying through dark galleries about their business of trying to make sense of why they hurried when their only reward was to bump into sharp black rocks. But the Great Grotto was quite something else.

High in its roof was a cleft, a fault in earth and rock that had allowed a single shaft of white sunshine to pierce through. The dazzling light mixed with the misty spray from the river combined to create an ever-present rainbow in that sacred place. Here, the life of the Fisher Clan was filled with light when they could relax and watch the river flow, or just gaze up at the sunlit rainbow and the Coke cans and the fishing floats that flowed through the Great Grotto, though the youngsters quickly made sense of the yellow plastic ducks that came bobbing by. These were eagerly rescued, for they made sturdy steeds to carry them through the watery tunnels and caverns of their world in search of unexplored places and mischief.

Yet, strangely, though the Fisher Clan knew that the river flowed down from the earth above, they had no idea where it flowed to. There had always been myths and stories about where the River of Dreams ended, but no one in their history had sought to find the truth. For the Fisher Clan had always been content as they were. Their part of the river provided them with everything they needed. So why worry about mysterious problems that might disrupt their contented lives? Let the river flow on and out of their sight, to where . . . they chose not to care.

Returning to the Great Grotto, Finn had one last emotional act to perform. Using the sharp barbs of his fishing harpoon he carved letters into the side of his new coracle. Then he straightened and shouted, his words echoing around the walls and cathedral roof of the grotto, causing the roosting bats to flutter in alarm.

'My father named his coracle *The Wave*,' he cried. 'Mine shall be known as *Wave the Second*, and may I complete his quest and come safe home as he did not. In his memory, and for the honour of the Fisher Clan, I shall sail forth across the world above to discover the secret beginnings of our sacred river. I, Finn, son of Finn, vow to do this in the name of my father, who never came home, and the dear people of the Fisher Clan. I shall not flag nor fail till—'

'How about me and your brothers and sisters?' yelled his mother, who was hiding behind a rock with her sobbing brood. She emerged, the kids in a clasped-hand chain behind her. 'Can't wait to see the back of us, eh?'

'It isn't like that at all, Mother,' Finn protested. 'You know I've been planning this quest for a long time. I was coming to say goodbye before I left.'

'Oh, Finn,' his mother wept, 'don't be your father all over again and never come home to us.'

'Who's going to teach us to catch fish and shrimps fresh from the river?' cried his brothers and sisters, accusingly. 'With you gone for ever, who can we turn to, you selfish Finn, you?'

'I have this great urge to explore the world above,' appealed Finn. 'Please try to understand, dear family. I feel the need to complete the expedition my father never came home from.'

'So that entitles you to wear his cap, I suppose?' snapped his mother. 'And name your coracle after his. Finn, I order you to return to our homely shelter in our cave immediately. I insist that you do your duty as a good son should. I won't tell you twice.'

'Come home and be our big brother again,' sobbed the kids. 'Don't desert us and die like Dad did.'

'All the distress you're causing because of a reckless whim!' scolded his mother. 'Your father had the same whim and look what happened to him! Who will provide for us when you go and never come back?'

'The clan will provide, Mother,' said Finn, determined not to have his mind changed. 'I must do what I must do.'

'Those were the famous last words of your father,' cried his mother. 'And now they are yours. Go if you must. And while you're enjoying your adventure, remember us, your family, plunged into grief.'

'You wicked, deserting Finn,' sobbed his brothers and sisters, as their mother led them home to light fish-oil candles, to pray for Finn and his silly quest.

'Goodbye,' shouted Finn, despairingly. 'I'll be back, I promise.'

There was no reply.

Moments later, and with a sad heart, Finn was hoisting his coracle on to his back to wear as a snail wore its shell for easy carrying. Brushing away his tears, he began the long and tiring climb upwards through the cave system to the world above. His plan was to bypass the violent dash of the River of Dreams where it poured underground, and launch his coracle in hopefully calmer reaches where the waters would be soothed and the paddling would be easier.

For one day and one whole night, he travelled up-river hugging the banks, for the current was still strong even here, beyond the narrow and furious gorge. From time to time he rested from the tiring paddling to consult his hastily scrawled map and to munch dried fish to boost his energy.

He was looking for a channel that flowed into the River of Dreams, the stream that the history books said snaked through the long valley from its source in the distant hills. Paddling on, Finn's hopes sank lower and lower. As yet, there was no sign of the small tributary he sought. Twice during that arduous journey he took sightings from the sky, the first from the sun, the second from the stars. Both the day and the night confirmed he was right on course, that he should have reached the branching course by now. Yet here was the puzzlement.

Why was he now paddling across a vast sea where no sea should be? Where was the stream? Where were the high valley hills? The doubts that had been nagging him for some time were becoming full-blown worries.

Bewildered and utterly spent, Finn curled up in the bottom of the coracle and fell fast asleep . . .

He was woken by the warmth of the rising orange sun on his face, though more startlingly by the harsh cries of a huge bird, buzzing and pecking at the sides of his drifting coracle. Angered, Finn jumped to his feet in time to see the bird flapping away through the morning haze. Shading his eyes with his hand, he scanned the boundless sea that seemed to mock his tiny boat with pushy, nudging waves.

Then, all at once, his searching eyes were taken

by the strange vessel sailing towards him. Soon, he could make out a host of faces lining the deck and peering down at him. The faces, though strangers, were clearly familiar. For they belonged to the People, not of course the Fisher Clan, but of the People nevertheless.

To Finn's relief they were waving and hailing in a friendly manner. Some were making urgent signs that he should paddle closer to their log. With renewed heart, Finn obeyed. It was at that exact moment that two small figures yelled as they lost control of the tiller. The log began to slew round in the water, presenting its stern to the furiously paddling Fisher Clan boy. With a crunch his fragile coracle struck the rearing side of the towed rowing-boat, the jail of Deadeye and his gang. Instantly the side of the boat was lined with faces. Soon they were spitting threats and insults at the hapless Finn below.

'Look, lads, we have a strange visitor served up in a giant stew-bowl,' mocked Deadeye, his good eye glinting with savage humour. 'Could it be that our jailers have sent us an early lunch? But he looks a bit tough, don't you think? Perhaps we should tenderise him before we boil him alive. Go to it, my rascals.'

No sooner ordered than done, and the gang began to snatch up anything to hand to hurl down on Finn and his coracle. The terrified Fisher boy could only cower and try to protect himself as the missiles rained down. Hemlock had thought of a quicker way to finish Finn off. With a few of his bully-boys, he swarmed down the makeshift rope-ladder to the bottom of the boat. Then, puffing under the weight, they climbed back on deck lugging two mysterious objects.

'One, two, three, heave!' yelled Hemlock. The can of Coke hurtled down, striking the side of the coracle. It burst, covering Finn in a sticky brown fizz.

It was the second weapon that did for the coracle. The plunging can of baked beans crashed through the bottom of the craft, smashing it to splintered bits.

Thrown into the water Finn sank like a stone, fighting to regain his senses. In his hand he clutched his fish harpoon as a straw to a drowning man. Rising, gasping for air, his instincts as a born swimmer took over. Shaking his dizzy head he struck out for the only hope he had, the log and the friendly faces aboard it.

Though weakened through injury, he made it. Still half-stunned and in pain, he wallowed in the wash of the log. Then he felt himself seized and hoisted upwards. After that, he was just dimly aware of flitting shapes and urgent voices, then nothing . . .

Fourteen

THE STARS DON'T TAKE SIDES

'Bring a lamp,' ordered Old Elder, peering down. 'And some healing bark oil. This youth is wounded and exhausted.'

'The pale sailor is more in need of some nourishing stew,' advised the grannies, bustling through the crush of watchers in a cloud of delicious steam. 'Spoon it down him piping hot for the best results. He'll soon be rosy-cheeked and chattering when our stew takes effect.'

Respecting the wisdom of the grannies, Fern crooked the stranger's head in her arm and began to force-spoon him. The stew had an amazing power to revive. Soon the patient was sitting up and licking the stew bowl clean. Yet not for one moment did Finn relax his grasp on his deadly barbed harpoon. Not even Robin was brave enough to try to take it from him.

'Would you like some more stew?' piped little Nettles. 'Because I know where to get it.'

'Away with you, young Nettles,' ordered Old Elder. 'Go and help the grannies in the kitchen with the washing-up.'

'You only treat me like a slave because I belong to the Nightshade Clan,' yelled Nettles. 'Why don't you just banish me to the prison-boat? Nothing could be worse than toiling in the grannies' hot kitchen.'

Still shouting, he was lifted from the deck and passed backwards over the heads of the crush, ending up in the kitchen where he got a scolding from the two grannies. Then, every eye and ear was again intent on the stranger, who was now showing signs of his need to talk.

'Where am I?' he asked, bewildered. 'What happened to my coracle? Why was I attacked for no reason at all? Who are you people, and why am I being held a prisoner?'

'You're not a prisoner,' Old Elder said, soothingly. 'You are our injured guest. You are aboard the ark of the Willow Clan and their friends. Your strange round boat was smashed to pieces by the evil Nightshade gang, whom we've imprisoned for many crimes. I'm afraid you sailed too close to them and bore the brunt of their hatred. But to introduce myself, I'm Old Elder of the Willow Clan, and who would you be?'

'I'm Finn, the son of Finn,' was the proud reply. 'And I belong to the Fisher Clan, who live in the caves beneath the world. I'm sailing on a great quest to find the source of the River of Dreams that flows through our Great Grotto.'

'Not sailing on a quest any more, though,' said Fern, sadly, 'because your comical coracle is now just bits of driftwood. And you looked so brave and attractive as you bobbed past

214

our ark with your white hair blowing in the breeze.'

'And your green eyes glowing with challenge,' sighed Pansy. Then she wrinkled her nose. 'What a pity you pong of fish close to.'

'It's plain that Finn is of the People,' said Robin, briskly, 'though clearly from no clan we know of. You speak of a quest to find the source of some river. Well, we aboard this ark are also bound on a quest, but in the opposite direction. As I am the fighting champion of the Willow Clan, I demand you explain yourself more. Forgive my arrow pointed at your heart but you could be an enemy with evil intent.'

'I'm not your enemy,' protested Finn. 'I'm just a simple explorer, like my father before me. I set out on my voyage to discover the source of the river that has, from the beginning of time, provided my Fisher Clan with their every need. My dream was to paddle against the odds and the currents to chart the exact spot where the River of Dreams begins, and bow down in homage at that place. Alas, now my coracle is gone, my journey is at an end. But even though I've failed, I'll always be proud that every paddle stroke I made was for the glory of my clan and in the name of my lost father.'

'Or in the name of your own naked ambition,' said Quickthorn, who wasn't keen on soaring words, even though he was a poet. 'I would like to ask some questions, which I doubt you'll know the answers to, Finn, son of Finn. But first I'll answer a few questions about myself, I being totally without ambition. Am I a poet of genius, as everyone says? No, I'm not. Am I a great leader of the People quietly waiting in the wings to snatch total power? No, I'm not. Do my looks and my charm excite females to flock around me? No, they don't. Those answers, Finn, explain why I'm completely without any ambition to be an extraordinary person. Now I'm going to fire a question at you, which you must answer with open honesty. Did you know when you set off on your quest that it would be a total failure and that you would end up being questioned by me?'

'I don't see the point of Quickthorn,' said Fern, irritated. 'He asks questions then answers them himself.'

'I think Quickthorn is a wonderful poet. The problem is we've heard none yet,' said Meadowsweet, disappointed. 'It seems he prefers to ask questions with no rhyme or reason in them. His questions do get boring.'

'In other words, you wish he'd shut up,' grinned Teasel. 'Well, you're about to get your wish, for Old Elder is about to speak.'

'Thank you, Quickthorn,' said Old Elder, confused. 'I'm sure your questions and answers have cleared up many doubts in many minds, but we must move on. If you'll all be silent I also have a question to ask our stranger guest that will prove if he is friend or foe. Finn, son of Finn, if you are a genuine explorer you must have set off with a map of some kind. Explorers always do. Can you produce such a map?'

'I can,' answered Finn. Reaching into his rough tunic, he produced what looked like a scrap of dried fishskin with marks scrawled on it. Ignoring the crowd, who were mostly holding their noses against the pong, he said, 'Here is my map, which I copied from one of our history books. I was faithfully following it when, sadly, everything went wrong.'

Old Elder took it and pored awhile. Then he looked up in surprise. 'No wonder you got lost, young Finn. You've been searching for a stream that winds through a long valley that no longer exists. For that stream and that valley were once our home and are now flooded by the great sea we float upon. This map shows the world as it once was, before the Humans opened their huge dam at the head of the valley. The source of the river you seek has been swallowed for ever, alas. Now what will you do, brave adventurer?'

'With the valley flooded and his coracle smashed, it's obvious,' said Pimpernel, sensibly. 'His only

218

solution is to join our quest, which is sailing on the course from which Finn came. He'll probably prove much more skilful going backwards than he was going forwards.'

'In plain words, in the direction of back to where you quested from,' said Fern, helpfully, to a very confused Fisher boy. She smiled happily. 'Which means you'll be needing a useful job aboard the ark. It so happens I need an assistant to help me look after the animal friends in our care. I'm sure Finn would be able to cope with a lady badger with a nervous breakdown and her son badger, who keeps threatening to run amok. I'm certain he would have the proper bedside manner to deal with dozing dormice, and would be kind but firm with tetchy squirrels. In my opinion, Finn will be perfect for the job I've just outlined, and he can start immediately.'

'I'd certainly do my best,' said Finn, bewildered, 'even though I don't know what a badger is.'

'Finn would be more use helping me with my duties,' snapped jealous Pansy. 'Many of my Nightshade Clan are still in shock after their near-drowning experience. I could do with Finn's help to carry my lamp while I tiptoe around, smoothing brows and tucking them in at night. As Finn has lived underground all his life his dreamy green eyes will be perfect for piercing through the dark, should the lamp splutter out. So, on your feet, Finn, we've work to do.'

'The two grannies have listened to every word, and they're frowning!' shouted Nettles, poking his sweaty head above deck. 'They also have a job for Finn. They are desperate for a washer-upper with longer and stronger arms than mine. They want Finn sent down to the kitchen with his sleeves rolled up to deal with the dirty stew bowls that are piling up and up. They say they might not be as pretty as Fern and Pansy, but filling bellies with stew is vitally important.'

'Explorers don't scrub stew bowls,' said Fern, annoyed.

'Nor do they fuss over cranky animals,' said Pansy, glaring.

It was quiet and thoughtful Sedge who came up with the best job offer for Finn. Urged on by his adoring family he spelled it out in such a sensible way that everyone was amazed they hadn't thought of it first.

'The situation is this,' he began. 'We on this ark are sailing in search of a dream. Finn was sailing the opposite way in search of his own. Now that his quest has turned turtle with the loss of his coracle and the news that the flood has swamped the source of the river he sought, I think he should throw in his lot with us. We must face the truth. No one knows where our sails are pushing us. Not even our magpie, soaring above, has a clue where we are. Would Finn consider the job offer of steering our ark from this endless sea into his River of Dreams where we can take our chances? Having failed in his own quest, will Finn help us to complete ours? Would Finn accept such a job offer, I wonder?'

'If he did, it would be a terrible blow to nursing,' said Pansy, shaking her glossy black head.

'Twice a blow to the care of helpless animals,' said Fern, regretfully.

'And how about the mountains of stew bowls that need washing up?' yelled little Nettles. 'I'm hoping to become an archer in Robin's band, so why is my ambition gurgling down the drain? I'll never ask for more again because the punishment is to wash up for the rest of your life. These days I choke on second helpings.'

'Will you steer us towards your river, Finn?' asked Old Elder. 'For this sea is wide and we are learners in the art of navigation.'

'Gladly,' said Finn, simply. Then his pale face clouded with fear. 'But only as far as the Great Grotto of my clan. From there on, you must travel alone. The ancient histories of my people warn that to sail to the end of the River of Dreams is to be plunged into a world of . . . of darkness . . . of—'

'Dreams,' finished Sedge, understanding the terror of the youth. 'Be calm, your courage is not in doubt, Finn, son of Finn. Steer us as far as your nerves will stand and we'll fend for ourselves from there on.'

'I stand ready to steer this ark,' cried Finn, sitting up, his sharp, harpoon spear brandished. 'From this moment on, your quest is mine, and I'll slay anyone who doubts my word.'

There were a couple of doubters. At the stern of the ark, Foxglove and Coltsfoot had been happily swinging on the huge tiller, steering a straight line across the sea. Then had heard Old Elder appoint the stranger Finn to be in charge of steering the ark and were firmly opposed to it.

'Finn will take this tiller over our dead bodies,' they cried. 'One minute he's nearly dead and the next minute he's alive and taking over our jobs. What does he know about steering in a straight line when he's still groggy? This is our tiller, and we'll defend it with our lives.'

'We're not demanding that Finn should take over the tiller,' said Old Elder, wearily, 'only that he's allowed to sit and watch and learn your skills.'

'That's different,' shouted Foxglove and Coltsfoot. 'Send Finn down to the stern and we'll teach him how to be an old sea-dog. But if he throws his weight about, we'll throw him over the side for the worms to nibble at!'

There was another commotion at the stern of the ark. The children, who had been given the task of keeping an eagle eye on the prison boat came racing with news, their faces grim and concerned.

'It's the Nightshade gang, Old Elder,' gasped the girl. 'At this time of night they should be fast asleep and dreaming about their release date. Instead they're burning the midnight oil with lots of shouting and laughter.'

'Yes, well, they were provided with an oil lamp

to brighten their darkness,' Old Elder replied. 'Even in prison they're entitled to cheer themselves up. The Willow Clan have never been cruel.'

'It's the triumphant way they're laughing,' said the worried boy. 'As though they're already celebrating their freedom.'

'I'm concerned about Dad's fishing locker in the boat,' said the friend. 'There's a lot of stuff in there that could be dangerous in the wrong hands.'

'Go back and keep watching and reporting,' ordered Old Elder. 'And take Finn, our new steerer, with you. Get to know him, for he's going to play an important role in the future of we on this ark.'

'That gang has got to be up to something,' said Robin, uneasily, as they watched the children and Finn hurry away.

'We can only stay alert and wait,' replied his leader.

'But wait for what?' said Fern, nervously . . .

The Nightshade gang had been busy for some hours. As dusk had fallen the previous day, they had started to mooch around the bowels of their prison. By the light from the oil lamp they soon discovered the fishing locker. Wrenching it open, they stared wide-eyed at the treasure trove of strange and useful-looking things revealed. Gazing, their warlike souls saw only a hoard of potential weapons as, with eager hands, they spilled them out. There, on the waterlogged planks of their prison, they scrabbled and pored over their glittering finds. They discovered that fishing-floats made excellent spears and lances when sharpened to a point. Fish-hooks hammered straight made vicious arrows for their bows, hastily carved from strong slivers of wood. They decided the coils of nylon line would be ideal for tying up the many prisoners they would take. It was a busy time for the gang as they sharpened and straightened and tested their new, modern weapons.

Toadflax remained apart. His interest had

been taken by the huge, strangely shaped object the others had ignored. Alone, he paced and thoughtfully examined the object from every angle, twanging its rubbery parts and gazing at the pouch-like section at its end. Then he turned his attention to the scattering of lead balls that had rolled from their upturned box. Slowly, because he had the slow-moving brain of a fool and a genius, an idea took quite long to form in his mind. But as he pondered, he smiled.

With their weapons ready, the gang sat in a circle in the light from the lamp and the cold beam of starlight above. All that remained was for Deadeye to tell them his plans and fire their lust for the coming battle.

'When our enemies are dead or captured we'll take over the ark,' he said, with relish. 'The survivors will become our slaves to do our bidding. Then we'll sail the sea as bloodthirsty pirates, swooping down on small settlements to loot and pillage and burn. The name and reputation of Deadeye's Raiders will soon make all the clans of the People quake in fear. All the riches in the world will be ours if we refuse to show mercy. For mercy equals weakness, and empires aren't built on softness.'

'No mercy!' shouted Hemlock. 'I'd sooner fall on my own spear than betray a spark of goodness in my soul.'

'But first we must capture the ark,' whispered Deadeye, gazing deep into every watching pair of eyes. 'My plan is to attack at dawn. We'll strike from where they'll least expect – across the anchor-line, taking them completely by surprise. Our lookout has informed me that the stern of the ark is undefended, save for two silly youngsters at the tiller and the Human children, who are fast asleep.'

'Oh, for the bloodbath to come,' yearned Hemlock, savagely. 'And with them out of the way I can seek out and plunge my spear deep into the back of Robin Prettyface!'

'Now to my plan,' said Deadeye. 'At dawn an advance party, led by Hemlock, will creep across the anchor-line and slaughter everyone at the stern of the ark. When that deed is done my son will hoot like an owl to signal the rest of us to cross over. Then we'll storm the ark like wild dervishes, cutting and thrusting without mercy. Old Elder will be left to me. I've been waiting a long time to bash his brains out. Now remember, the advance raid must take place in complete silence otherwise surprise will be lost.'

'It's the swaying anchor-line that worries me,' said a member of the advance party. 'With steady ground under my feet I'm a hero, but on that swinging rope above water I'm a whining coward. It was only the pricking point of a sword that coaxed me here in the first place.'

'One whine while crossing the rope will be the last sound you ever make,' warned Deadeye. 'I'll be watching out for lily-livered cowards. If you must topple from the rope then do it silently.

And don't splash when you enter the water, for sound carries.'

'May I speak, Chief?' asked Toadflax, approaching and looking pleased with himself. 'I think I've got the perfect secret weapon that will take all the hard work out of fighting battles.'

'Not lumps of wood with bits stuck on the side again?' snarled Hemlock. 'Must we listen to the ramblings of this idiot? We're about to fight a great battle and all Toadflax thinks about is making toys. I don't know how he became a member of our gang in the first place. He was never near cruel enough.'

'Let Toadflax speak,' interrupted Deadeye, a rare hint of a smile on his face. 'I sometimes like to hear him talk nonsense, it relaxes me. Especially at times like this, when my plans are laid and I need some small amusement. Let the foolish one speak and give us all a laugh.'

'Thanks, Chief,' said Toadflax, relieved. 'While you're still smiling, I'd like to make a request about the brilliant secret new weapon I've invented. The problem is, it's very heavy and I'll need help to mount it on the bow up top. It needs to be fixed there for the best destructive results. If you could spare a few strong arms to help me carry it up the ladder . . .'

'Why not?' said Deadeye, still smiling. He nodded at two of the gang, who jumped smartly to their feet. Instantly his face twisted to become its familiar evil mask again. His knuckles whitened as he gripped the club that would dash out the brains of his arch-enemy, Old Elder.

'Let's roar our battle song,' cried Hemlock. 'And let us smile in triumph as we sing it. For it's in the stars that tomorrow will be our day.'

'Pray that those stars shine on us tomorrow night,' murmured Deadeye, to the spark of doubt he felt in his troubled soul. 'For if they shine in favour on my enemies, it'll mean the end of me.'

As Toadflax and his helpers huffed and puffed up and down the rope-ladder, the gang burst into their raucous song, their fierce eyes glowing in the light of the lamp that slowly dimmed and spluttered to gutter away. Then, too, the cold, unfeeling stars faded, to make way for the red sun to rise, to dominate the coming day.

Fifteen

THE BATTLE FOR THE ARK

Save for the slapping wallow of the ark through the water, all was quiet aboard the vessel. Exhausted from hours of watching for danger, the children had fallen asleep. Curled up beside the tiller, Coltsfoot and Foxglove also slumbered.

Finn, the Fisher boy, seemed to be the only soul awake as he peered into the night, steering the ark back along the course of his outward-bound journey. He was quite content. Though sad that his quest had failed so miserably, he was glad to help the Willow Clan people achieve theirs. Alone, and in charge of the gently bucking tiller, his sense of adventure had fully returned.

Glancing to see that the sleepers were well, he adjusted his father's old fishing-cap to a rakish angle and squinted at the stars to take a bearing on his position. He was satisfied. He reckoned that another half day's sailing would bring the ark within sight of the channel that branched from this dreary sea. Then would come the exhilarating breakneck plunge through the narrow gorge, and he would be almost home.

Lulled by the rocking motion, he was suddenly alerted by a brilliant beam of orange light in his eyes as the sun began to rise above the horizon. Then, suddenly, he was listening to a strange creaking sound coming from behind him. Jumping to his feet, he spun round, his harpoon poised.

Immediately he was fighting for his life, as Hemlock and his advance party rushed him. A jabbing spear pierced his shoulder, sending him reeling back. He managed to yell, to rouse the sleepers and urge them to hurry away to safety. Then he was parrying more vicious thrusts and stabbing back with his razor-sharp harpoon. To his surprise and grateful relief, he found the Human boy and the friend fighting gamely beside him. Blood flowed and cries were loud on the morning air. Despite their bravery, the three were forced back by their savagely grinning enemies.

The odds against them quickly increased, as over the swaying rope came the main force, with Deadeye in the lead. The gallant three had no choice but to break off the fight and flee to join Robin and his band who, alarmed by the din, had formed themselves into a battle force, bows, swords and spears at the ready as they began to advance against their ancient and sworn enemies.

Before the two sides could clash, an astonishing

thing happened. First, everyone heard a strange noise, a juddering, twanging sound followed by whistling, as if the air were being ripped apart by some terrible force. Suddenly, huge leaden balls began to plummet down among Deadeye and his gang, felling and injuring and causing panic in the ranks of the invaders.

Toadflax and his strong helpers had succeeded in erecting the secret weapon on the bow of the prison-boat. Securely lashed into position with lots of fishing-line it reared, huge and menacing, against the starry sky. Beside it was heaped a pile of ammunition that Toadflax had chosen from the scattered contents of the fishing locker. As Hemlock and his raiding party began to sidle and shuffle along the swaying anchor-line, Toadflax ordered his helpers to prepare to fire. Obediently he was waiting for the dawn truly to break, the moment that Deadeye had ordered the main attack to begin. As the orange sun rose and Deadeye and his force hurried across the rope, so Toadflax and his secret weapon went to war, hence the juddering, twanging sound and the whistle of missiles flying through the air. Pleased to see his invention working so perfectly, Toadflax ordered another salvo to be fired . . .

There was a stunned bewilderment aboard the ark. Neither side had any idea of what was happening. Was the mysterious barrage a warning from on high that war among the clans of the People would not be tolerated? Yet the Willow Clan and their friends had never wanted this battle. Could that be the reason that only Deadeye and his gang were being picked out to suffer the rain of heavenly missiles? As they had started the fighting, it certainly seemed like it. Then a second salvo came whistling in, completely missing the ark, to shower harmlessly into the sea. It was clear that whoever was responsible could only aim straight the first time.

While both sides tried to puzzle out the mystery, the bloodied and bruised friend gave a shout and pointed at the bow of the prison-boat. 'Look! Who'd believe it? That's my dad's catapult!' he yelled. 'The one he uses to fire ground-bait into the fishing-swim when he's angling for chub. Some great genius has rigged it up to make a guided-missile launcher!'

'Be quiet and face your front,' ordered Robin. He turned to his readied band. 'The enemy have been dealt a miraculous blow and are in confusion. Prepare to advance. Archers, draw your bows. Spear-men, make every thrust count! We are defending our ark and our people in a righteous cause. And now, forward into the final battle against the foe.'

Shocked and battered, but unbowed, Deadeye and Hemlock gathered together their unwounded forces and charged, yelling their battle song, weapons at the ready, to thrust and rip and bludgeon. Evil they might be, but they could fight with the best when the heat of battle was upon them.

As the sides clashed, more fell dead and injured.

Little Nettles, who yearned to be an archer, had dashed up from the kitchen and was laying about him with a cooking pot. He quickly learned about the seriousness of battle when he was thrown to the deck and trampled on. For there was no quarter asked or given.

The Nightshade gang were fighting for total control of the ark, the Willow Clan and their friends for their very existence. Even poets like Teasel, Meadowsweet and Quickthorn entered the fray. For they knew that verse and freedom of speech would be stifled if Deadeye and his gang won the day.

On the sidelines sat Sedge and his anxious family, while above the magpie dug his claws into his oaken perch and prayed for a just outcome. He and faithful Sedge could not intervene. The battle was between clans of the People, a private, tribal matter. It was not their business to interfere. To their relief the fight was going the way they hoped. As if sensing defeat, Deadeye had broken away from the skirmish. Bloodied and panting, his good eye searched for the one he most hated and had vowed to kill.

Old Elder, with Fern and Pansy beside him, was guarding the hatch that led below to where many innocents huddled in fear. Spying him, Deadeye launched himself with a savage yell at his old enemy. For one brief moment, Old Elder gazed into Deadeye's crazed eye before his skull was crushed by a mighty blow from a club. Deadeye was just about to despatch Fern and Pansy with more brutal blows when he was tapped on the shoulder from behind. Whirling about, his single eye stared at the gleaming spear-tip, the last thing he would ever see. At the same moment, he heard the last words he would ever hear in his long and wicked life.

'Go quickly . . . to where you belong,' said Pimpernel, driving his blade deep into an evil heart. 'And don't hope to find forgiveness where I send you.'

So died two leaders of the People, one good, one bad.

And with their deaths the verve and passion of the battle seemed to drain away in tiredness. Suddenly, there seemed no point in fighting any more. The Willow Clan and their friends had won the day, but at great cost to all who had taken part. Among the Nightshade gang only one refused to lay down his arms. With the death of his father, he was now leader in his own right. He brushed away a tear, though it might have been sweat. He knew that to survive he needed to assert his authority in the eyes of his defeated gang or he was nothing. He did what he knew he had to do. He accepted defeat, then issued a challenge he knew could not be refused.

Hemlock spoke. 'We submit to your superior strength, proud Robin,' he said, leaning on his bloodied spear. 'The day is yours. I've lost a father, you a leader and many more besides. My comrades are now your prisoners. Treat them well, for they did only the bidding of my father and me. As for myself, I ask you to recall the day when we challenged each other at

'With just this tiny dagger, I'll defend this ark against the evil you represent, for right is on my side.'

There were a few weak cheers from Hemlock's depleted throng, and an uproar of protest from the rest of the circle of onlookers. What in the world was Robin up to, risking precious lives because of his pride? the whisper ran. Didn't he know that pride usually came before a fall?

'He's no need to fight Hemlock at all,' said Pansy, bewildered. 'The gang are captives and with no legs to stand on.'

'I intend to write a great epic poem about this tragic fight,' said Meadowsweet, quite awed by the occasion. 'If Robin wins, it will ring with valour and joy. If Hemlock wins and I'm thrown into prison I'll scratch mournful verses on the wall.'

'And I'll help with the rhyming,' teased Teasel. Then he was serious. 'But don't let's fret. Though Robin seems a fool just yet, his luck will hold, I'll bet.'

'Don't will yourself to death, Robin,' wept

many in the crowd, 'for you will us to death, too. When you fall before Hemlock's huge spear, our lives won't be worth living.'

'Want to back down, Robin Prettyface?' sneered Hemlock, hefting the spear and slipping his arm through the large, protecting shield. 'But of course you won't, for you'd rather die than humble your pride before me. And die you will, for your foolishness saw to that. You should have tried to kill me in the heat of battle, as my father and your Old Elder died. Now it's too late. Now we fight with every advantage on my side, thanks to your stupid honour and my unfair choice of weapons. And no one will lift a finger to help you when I spear you through. For, as you agreed, the winner will be the new leader of this ark. Before I despatch you, Robin Proudheart, imagine the cries and the suffering of your Willow Clan when I begin my harsh rule.'

'Let's get on with it!' cried Robin, brandishing his puny dagger. 'And let right and justice triumph.'

Immediately Hemlock jabbed with his long spear, drawing blood from Robin's arm. As Robin desperately tried to close, to use his dagger, Hemlock stabbed him again, then brought his heavy shield smashing down on Robin's head, sending him reeling. As Hemlock rushed with his spear poised to finish his opponent, so a familiar juddering, twanging sound was heard, followed by a whistling noise that caused everyone to fall in terror to the deck. Suddenly, down from the blue sky, plummeted a single leaden shot to score a direct and devastating hit.

Moments before the single combat fight had begun, Toadflax, standing beside his secret weapon on the bow of the ark, ordered his last missile to be loaded into the pouch of the launcher.

'Now, lads,' he cried to his two helpers, 'our first salvo was a brilliant success and caused great damage aboard the enemy ark. Sadly, our second salvo was a dud, due to bad aiming and too much pressure on the left-hand side of the twanger. We have one shot left, so let's make it count, lads. Let it strike like a thunderbolt upon the head of our greatest enemy. Ready, steady . . . fire!'

On the ark, everyone was hugging the deck, their ears covered as they awaited the attack from the sky. All except Robin and Hemlock, who continued their grim battle, oblivious to everything else. The lead ball struck. Cautiously rising, the crowd uncovered their eyes to see Robin still clutching his unused dagger and looking astonished. At his feet lay the crumpled and lifeless body of Hemlock, the lead missile still rocking beside his crushed head.

There was more confusion, caused by a commotion at the stern of the ark. Along the swaying anchor-line came Toadflax and his gunnery team, cheering and whooping as they gained the deck. They were certain they had scored a perfect strike, and were eager to be hailed as heroes by Deadeye and the gang.

Then they saw the carnage the secret weapon

had wreaked. Not damage to their enemies but to the gang they had loyally supported. Toadflax looked stunned as he gazed at the body of Deadeye, wept a tear to view the crushed head of Hemlock, burst into sobs when he saw his dead and wounded comrades, the brothers in arms he had lived and sung with. Toadflax realised that he and his awesome weapon were responsible for the defeat of his gang. He had begun his career with the Nightshade mob as the butt of their jokes. Now he was ending it as their destroyer.

'I only built my weapon to overpower our enemies,' he cried, in despair. 'Instead I've killed and wounded my own. Never again will I dabble with science now that I know the misery it can cause. I beg the Willow Clan to kill me and my genius before we lay waste the whole world.'

'No, misguided Toadflax,' said wounded Pimpernel, gently. 'You and your genius did what you set out to do, to destroy the enemies of our

Nightshade Clan. Soon you'll come to understand that the ones who led us were our greatest
enemies. Now they're dead, never again will
they strut and bully you into wickedness. I now
address Robin, the new leader of this ark, for I
have some requests to make.'

'Make them, brave Pimpernel,' replied Robin,
wincing from his wounds. 'If they're reasonable,
I'll certainly grant them.'

'My requests are these,' said Pimpernel. 'That
the surviving members of the gang are treated
kindly. Now that the evil spell of Deadeye and
Hemlock has been broken, I'm sure they can
become useful members of this ark, as I and
Pansy, as Quickthorn and small Nettles, have.
And that everyone aboard this ark can bury their
anger to work together to complete the quest we
are bound on.'

'They are my thoughts, too,' said Robin, as Fern
nodded her agreement. 'Make the survivors of
the Nightshade gang welcome and comfortable,
Pansy. Bind up their wounds and walk among

them with your lamp until they're healed in body and soul.'

'The grannies in the kitchen also have a request to make!' yelled tiny Nettles, poking his battle-bruised head above the deck. 'Their ears being sharp, they've heard there's a scientific genius aboard the ark called Toadflax. They insist that he's sent down to the kitchen to solve the problem of hot cooking-pot handles. They say they're fed up with shouting, "Ouch!"'

'Heat-proof handles is the answer,' said Toadflax, happily rubbing his chin as he thought. 'It's all a question of insulation. Tell the grannies I'm on my way down . . .' and away he hurried, excited to get to grips with a new problem that involved pots of peace, not missiles of war.

Finn came hurrying from below, where his wounds had been hastily dressed. Glancing anxiously at the sky, he spoke urgently to Robin. 'The wind is rising and we're sailing off course,' he said. 'I must get back to the tiller before we miss the channel that will take us through the gorge and into the River of Dreams. If you could pile on more sail, Captain Robin?'

'Make more sail!' yelled Robin, sending every sailor scurrying to pull on ropes and swarm aloft in nautical style.

'Don't worry about the tiller, Robin,' cried Foxglove and Coltsfoot, from the stern end of the ark. 'We're totally in charge again. Finn isn't needed here. He should have stayed below, resting in the sickroom in the tender care of Pansy and her lamp. We're now steering three degrees to port . . . or is it ten degrees to starboard?'

'No, please, no!' cried Finn, limping back to the tiller as fast as he could. 'I told you to steer a straight course until I returned.'

'We demand to know when this quest will be over,' stormed the Chief Squirrel, swarming down through a tangle of ropes and flapping material. 'How many more times are you going to juggle with the sails? First you hoist them, then you lower them, then you reef or furl them. Why can't you make up your minds? And I must warn you, Robin, we squirrels are rock-bottom on nuts at this moment in time. Is there any chance of reaching our new paradise before we all starve to death?'

'Not much longer now,' said Robin, soothingly. 'Most of our troubles are behind us, I'm certain. Tell all your friends to keep their chins up for a while longer.'

'Oh, they'll love that!' fumed the squirrel, vanishing back among the sails.

'My mum's weeping again,' warned the son badger. 'And her paws are tightly clenched, which is a very bad sign. It's all this fighting and noise that makes her nerves jangle. As for my dad, he just lies and snores and leaves the worrying about my mum to me. As soon as we get to the glorious new valley, I'm going to gather some anti-trembling herbs to calm her frantic twitching. So, sail this ark as fast as you can, Willow Clan. For if my mum doesn't get some treatment soon I'm going to run amok and leave a trail of shocking damage in my wake.'

'Oh, do keep the noise down,' sighed one of the sleepy dormice poking his head from his snug home. 'We're trying to lose ourselves in peaceful dreams in here. We hate it when the harsh world intrudes into our snoozing one.'

'Don't worry, welcome stowaways,' cried Robin, ignoring the pain from his wounds and blinking back tears. 'The dream Old Elder fired us with will be realised, I promise you. We'll pursue his dream unto the end of time itself, and further if a spark of hope remains . . .'

Then came a sad task to perform. The dead, good or bad, were treated with equal reverence. Wrapped in barkcloth shrouds, they were lowered with grave respect, into the sea. There were no angry words from the Willow Clan as Dead-eye and Hemlock were afforded the same honour as their own. The few remaining members of their wicked gang looked silently on, sorry and humbled now. As the slipping to rest of

Old Elder took place, Grandma Willow trudged from below and buried her face in her apron as her life-partner vanished beneath the water. Grandma Nightshade stood comforting her, she also with much to grieve about, for blood was blood, no matter how evil. Fern stood alone, her cheeks streaming tears. Robin stood head bowed, contemplating the awesome task that had descended upon him. As the last of the dead were slid into the sea he raised his head and spoke for all.

'Good or bad, the ones we've laid to rest were all of the People,' he said. His words were echoed by everyone in that sombre gathering.

Then it was back to work, for life and time moved ever forward towards new things. There would be quiet moments enough to grieve in private. But for now there was a new valley to be sought and claimed, and that was worry enough. Everyone was soon back at their tasks, intent on bringing the ark into the haven they knew not where. For a while Robin paced the deck, deep in thought. Every so often he would lift his gaze and stare at a certain spot. At the rough-hewn seat of his revered leader, Old Elder . . .

'Claim it, Robin braveheart, new leader of the Willow Clan,' said a soft voice. It was Sedge. 'Take your deserved place and achieve what Old Elder didn't live to do. Sail this ark and all the trusting souls aboard into that wonderful valley that surely awaits our coming!'

'With the help of Finn and the faith you have in me, I will,' said Robin, deeply moved.

'Land . . . land . . .' cried the magpie, zooming in to perch, quite out of puff. 'I've spied a stream not far ahead that branches from this sea. Quite calm enough at first, until it dives out of sight between two rocky cliffs. Then it appears again to flow calm again, before suddenly vanishing underground. Very strange and scary in my opinion, but yours is a wiser head than mine, my leader Robin.'

Robin hurried to the stern of the ark to find

Finn sitting at the tiller and smiling, despite his wounds. On either side of him sat Foxglove and Coltsfoot, their small hands also grasping the tiller, their cheeks weathered and their eyes squinting against the sun and the spray in the fashion of all expert helmsmen. Robin spoke urgently, anxiously.

'Our Scout Magpie has brought news of land, Finn. And about a branching stream he's spied. But his report worries me. The stream seems to duck and dive in a most perculiar way. He actually said it disappears twice. Have we cause to worry, I wonder?'

'He'll be talking about the gorge,' said Finn, still smiling happily. 'The rapids will be tough to negotiate but I think we'll beat them. As for the second disappearance, that's the home strait for me. But warn everyone aboard, soon I'll be heeling the ark over in order to enter the channelling stream. It's the rapids in the gorge we must be wary of. One false swing of the tiller could smash us to peices on the rocks. I suggest you order everything battened down and for everyone to be ready for a bumpy ride and a thorough soaking.'

'I'll do that at once, Finn,' said Robin, turning to dash back. 'And we thank you deeply for helping us succeed in our quest while your own ended in disaster.'

'Don't worry about Finn's outward-bound failure, Robin,' shouted Coltsfoot and Foxglove. 'He's much more suited to homeward-bound ones. He's positive he knows his way home to his Great Grotto. And we're at his side, on both sides of him, in case his hand trembles on the tiller and steers us backwards.'

'Attention, crew!' cried Robin. 'Batten down everything then stand ready as the ark enters the dangerous gorge. While you're waiting for further orders, dance a few jigs and tie some knots in bits of rope. Just stay alert and ready to spring into action at a moment's notice.'

'Aye, aye, Captain Robin!' roared the trusty crew.

All of a sudden, the ark was heeling over as Finn steered into the narrow channel that branched from the dreary, seemingly endless sea . . .

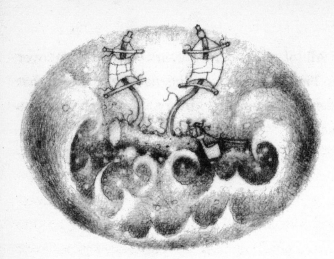

Sixteen

THE RIVER OF DREAMS

The channel seemed ominously calm to the worried sailors. As the battered and sail-reefed vessel drifted down it, the hills on either side grew taller, the lazing waters narrower. Soon the waterway was joined by another stream, and then another, all combining to become the River of Dreams. Coasting peacefully along, the

People aboard were able to lounge and admire the grassy views and the colours of autumn trees and flowers as they drifted by. The calm and peace were not to last.

'White water ahead!' yelled the magpie, scouting and spying on the wing.

Soon, Finn and his two young helpers were wrestling with the tiller as the ark plunged into a froth of white spray and somehow righted itself again. The ark was entering the dreaded gorge.

'Rocks on the port bow!' cried Sedge, his eyes scanning for such dangers.

'Swinging to starboard!' shouted Finn, pushing the tiller hard over, lifting his two small friends off their feet as they clung on for grim death.

Now was a time of fear and tension for the People aboard, as they bravely battled yet another hazard that threatened their journey to a new and better life. Though they had endured much, not one soul complained as they did what they could to comfort the old and young through the nightmarish, plunging ride among the turbulent crashing waters of the gorge. Sickened and frightened, they managed a weak cheer as the waters calmed and widened, and the ark emerged from the towering cliffs to sail into sunshine again.

The relief to be out of the gorge didn't last long. All at once, the ark gave a shuddering lurch as Finn pushed over the tiller and steered directly at an outcrop of rocks. Suddenly, they were sailing into the mouth of an enormous cave and down into the bowels of the earth. It was an eerie place of dripping walls and echoing caverns. They had entered the world of Finn and his Fisher Clan people.

As Finn skilfully steered the ark through the maze of gloomy tunnels, the People said little as they gazed about in awe. The only sounds to be heard were the lap of water, the scrape of tall masts on low ceilings and the echoing whimper of a frightened child. There was also a muted bumping noise against the sides of the ark. It was the sound of discarded plastic trash the Humans had dumped in the rivers and streams in order to make room for newer plastic trash. For the Fisher Clan, much of this rubbish was treasure to be netted and sorted for usefulness. The River of Dreams had always been a source of bounty for them. It provided the fish that made up their diet, and gifts a-plenty from the generous world above. The Fisher Clan worshipped the river, and rightly so.

Then the ark emerged from the last dark tunnel and sailed into the dazzling light of the Great Grotto. The amazed passengers gazed around this huge cathedral-like place, and wondered where the light was coming from. Then they raised their heads and saw the single shaft of fierce sunshine piercing down through the fault in the rock above. The light seemed to bounce from the surface of the river to shower every corner of this magical hall with near daylight.

Robin and Fern and everyone else rushed to crowd the deck, to stare and gasp at the extraordinary scenes of everyday life that were going on everywhere. Unnoticed as yet, they were able to observe this strange community, whose motto seemed to be constant busyness combined with enjoyment. There were folk fishing and hauling their catches on to golden beaches, others sorting the latest items of treasure to build into altars, and fires spitting fat, as fish and shrimps sizzled on the beach barbecues. A group of pale-skinned, green-eyed children swam and paddled their small coracles in the shallows, while higher up the beach a circle of elders sat whittling and carving, and shaping the bounty from the river into harpoons, cooking pots and toys for the young.

Then their peace was shattered as the huge, ponderous ark was spied approaching. There were cries of fear and a frantic dash for the safety of the caves as the ark, steered by Finn and the youngsters, moored gently off the now deserted beach.

Finn left the tiller and hurried to join an anxious Robin on the deck. He addressed his hidden people, his words echoing round the Great Grotto.

'It is I, Finn, son of Finn, returned from my wanderings,' he shouted. 'Though I've failed in my quest to find the source of the River of Dreams, I've come home with my head held high. For on my travels I discovered a race of our relatives, who live their lives above the earth. The folk you see aboard this ark are also of the People. Their valley has been destroyed by a great flood, and they wish to sail through the Great Grotto and onwards to find the end of the River of Dreams, where they believe lie their hopes for a new life. As they are of the People, I feel we are bound to help them. Where is our Fisher Clan leader, Old Silverscale? I beg to speak with him.'

From a small cave high on the beach emerged a noble figure with snowy-white hair and piercing green eyes. He was clad in a glittering fishskin cloak. In his pale, gnarled hand, he carried a viciously barbed harpoon. He advanced down the sands, a retinue of other ancients surrounding him. Though he looked all-powerful and warlike, his voice was calm and measured.

said Robin, 'but now that our valley has been destroyed by the flood we must find another one or perish.'

'It is good that the Fisher Clan are not alone in the world,' nodded Old Silverscale, 'and we will help you all we can. But your plan to sail on down the River of Dreams troubles me. Not even our great explorer, the father of Finn, would have attempted such a perilous and unknown journey. And who would guide you there? No, Robin, there are places best left unsought. My advice is to travel no further and stay with us as our welcome guests for as long as you wish.'

'We thank you, but we cannot,' said Robin. 'If we stayed here, we would soon yearn to feel the wind in our hair and the hot sun on our faces. We beg you, Old Silverscale, allow us to travel on, for we have a hope in our hearts that will not die until we sail to the end of the River of Dreams.'

'Then sail on, brave Robin,' replied Old Silverscale, sadly. 'Go with our blessing, and good luck.'

'Bless me, too, Old Silverscale,' said Finn, determined. 'I've decided to sail on with my new friends, for the lust to discover new places still burns inside me. If I could not complete my own quest, then I'll help the Willow Clan complete theirs. I need to do this for my dead father to be proud of me.'

'We, the living, are proud of you, Finn,' said gentle Old Silverscale. 'And when you don't return we'll carve your name on the altar we built for your father. You'll remain in our memory as a hero who lost his life helping others.'

'Not in my memory he won't!' cried Finn's mother, scurrying out of a cave and dragging her bawling children behind her. 'Finn's just come home from one hopeless quest and now he wants to dash off on another. Who's going to feed our hungry mouths when Finn is dead like his father? Old Silverscale, I beg that you order my son to stay at home and catch fish and shrimps, as a proper son should. He has no right sailing off and leaving a starving family behind, as his father did before him. Why is my family cursed with unreliable providers?'

'We implore Finn not to leave us again,' sobbed his brothers and sisters. 'We need him to catch us fresh fish and give us hugs every day. We want him to stay home and live a humdrum life like other Fisher boys. We beg him to settle down and be a proper, caring brother to us.'

'I'm torn between emotions,' cried Finn, anguished. 'I love my family but I must have challenge in my life. I need to live on the edge of mystery and danger as my father did.'

'You've certainly inherited his selfish, wanderlust dreams,' shrilled his angry mother. 'He never cared what become of us left home alone,'

'What shall I do, Old Silverscale?' Finn implored. 'In your wisdom, please help me to decide.'

'If the longing to explore still grips your soul, then go, Finn, son of Finn,' said the old one, nodding gravely. 'Live your life on the edge of tragic adventure, for our stay-at-home world is not for you. As for your family they'll be well looked after while your bones whiten on some terrible shore. They'll get all the fish and the hugs they need from our close-knit Fisher Clan. And remember, when you and your new friends sail on down the River Of Dreams, fear no evil . . . for our blessings travel with you. Goodbye, Finn, son of Finn, and may your bones wash ashore in some sacred place at the end of the world you seek . . .'

There then arose a mighty chorus of voices from the surrounding caves as the Fisher-folk mourned in song the loss and the death of Finn before his leaving of them. As the ark slipped her moorings and drifted into the first dark tunnel on the waves of the River Of Dreams, a host of voices rose up to the ringing heights of the Great Grotto . . .

'None but the brave dare go
In quest of dreams
Where cold dark waters flow.
Sail with the blessings of your kin

Fate keep you safe,
Finn, son of Finn.'

The song and the voices faded away as the ark vanished into the darkness, the final notes echoing sadly away.

Finn's grim-faced mother had no time for singing. As far as she was concerned her eldest son was a good-for-nothing runaway. But she and her weeping children were soon smiling again as they tucked into a huge meal of fish and shrimps and watercress generously provided by their neighbours. Perhaps life without Finn wouldn't be too bad after all . . . ?

The River Of Dreams flowed like a glistening black snake through the maze of caves. First it twisted this way, then that, causing desperate moments for the frantically steering Finn, Colts-foot and Foxglove. The journey through that gloomy place seemed set to go on for ever for the tired and anxious passengers aboard. Perhaps it was a malicious trick of the river that it did go on for ever through this terrible place? Perhaps they were already enraptured by the river and were deep in a dream from which they would never wake?

I spy light ahead!' cried the magpie, excitedly. 'Only a pinpoint, but certainly light.'

'And coming nearer and brighter!' yelled Sedge, peering forward over the bows. There was a rush to see, everyone eager to believe that the long nightmare of darkness was over . . .

It was.

Suddenly, the ark burst forth from the last tunnel into the blue skies and sunshine of a new and beautiful day. There were gasps of delight and cheers, as the folk aboard feasted their light-starved eyes on the sights that greeted them. Now the ark was lazily drifting on the silver waters of a stream that wound through a long valley. The heights on either side were crowned with oak and other trees, all jostling to grow big and strong in the rich brown soil.

Carpets of bluebells graced the clearings among the trees, while daffodils swayed in thick swathes in the water meadows that sloped down to the stream. And the clear spring air was filled with the joyous sound of birdsong.

This, surely, was the promised valley at the end of the River of Dreams, a place that had never known, would never know, the dread of Human presence. This was the valley the voyagers had suffered so much to find. The new home for which many had died that others might reach it. Gazing at the beauty all around them, the Willow Clan and their friends bowed their heads in accord and offered thanks for the wondrous gift bestowed on them.

THE VALLEY THAT TIME
FORGOT

The battered ark cruised in to anchor in the
shallows of the dreaming stream beneath a great
oak tree. It was a time of emotion for everyone
aboard as they realised that their quest was at
an end. The rugged craft that had carried them
so far would not be forgotten. The voyage of

the ark would enter into history and legend, as future folk came to gaze at the rotting hulk that had sailed their forebears across the sea in search of this new valley. But for now there was a whole fresh world to explore and delight in.

The People were soon clambering ashore in droves, desperate to feel firmness under their feet instead of the constant rocking motion they had endured for so long. Already the carpenters had hurried off with their tools, intent on making the huge oak into a home fit for heroes. Yet was there need any more to hide in the trees? For of their ancient Human enemy there was no sign.

It was Sedge who said it, though such was the bustle and excitement that his was a lone and unlistened-to voice. He said it again, but louder. But he was speaking to himself, as the sick and wounded began to file from below to stretch their cramped limbs and sniff the fresh air of this beautiful place. Especially happy were the long-downtrodden people of the Nightshade Clan. The tyranny of Deadeye was over, and they were their

'So our quest has sailed us back through time,' said Fern, awed. 'Our faith in our dreams must have brought this about.'

'And with not a Human footprint to spoil it all,' said Robin. 'Our wishes have been granted by a kind flow of water.'

'Talking about wishes being granted,' interrupted the Chief Squirrel, swarming down through the forest of masts and tattered sails, 'my committee and I have been scanning this new valley from aloft. We've spied out a grove of trees that groan beneath the weight of all kinds of nuts. We are therefore giving notice that we're deserting this ark in order to fill our empty bellies. We may return for a Grand Meeting, or we may not. So, all-conquering Robin, expect us when you see us,' and he bounded ashore, his large following eager on his swift heels.

Robin, Fern and Sedge exchanged smiles. How peaceful to be rid of that quarrelsome bunch. They hoped that the nuts in the grove were plentiful enough to keep the squirrels occupied for a long time to come. Grand Meetings called by squirrels were so boring when there was no need for them.

Sedge slipped over the side with his family, intent on building a new home in the inviting sandy bank.

Robin and Fern were content to gaze around at the beauty of the valley and listen to the shouts of joy as their family and friends discovered new wonders in this safe and welcoming land.

Just then, the two were tapped on their shoulders by a very strong paw.

'First of all, I wish to complain about the voyage,' said the young badger, his parents behind and waiting to be led ashore. 'The constant rocking of the ark and the din of clashing swords did my mum's nerves no good at all. Her health is now back where it started, in desperate need of anti-trembling herbs. However, the food wasn't bad, such as it was. You'll be wondering why I didn't run amok all the times I threatened to. Well, it was because I knew you were deep-down kind and doing your best, such as it was. Me and my parents are now going on a long, relaxing buzzle through the fields of buttercups we see yonder. Then, when our nerves and short tempers are healed, we intend to dig a deep sett and live calm and balanced lives for ever after. We'll never forget the kindness you showed us in our time of crisis. You could have thrown us over the side of the ark and been done with our moans and groans, but you didn't.

So, Robin and Fern, my father thanks you, my mother thanks you, and I thank you, too. May you always live in peace and tranquillity, as we intend to do,' and he and his shambling parents plodded away to find peace in the valley.

'We've brought all our precious cargo safely home,' said Robin, deeply moved. 'Let the ending of our quest be for ever celebrated in the name of Old Elder, who never lived to see his dream come true.'

'May my grandfather . . . may the slain, who

were of the People, rest in peace under the sea,' said Fern, with tear-filled eyes.

Then she was startled to feel another tap on her shoulder. This one was feather soft and hesitant. Turning, she and Robin saw two sleepy eyes and a twitching nose poking from a knot-hole in the main-mast. It was one of the stowaway dormice, blinking in the bright sunshine of a new and perfect day.

'Why have we stopped sailing?' He yawned. 'Dreams don't stop in the middle of a journey but at the end of one. Why don't you all go back to sleep and be patient? The dream will end when it's ready.'

'But it *has* ended,' said Fern. 'Pop out and see for yourself. We're back in our valley as it was before the Humans came to destroy it. Pinch yourself and breathe the sweet air of our new home, dozy old dormouse.'

'*Pinch* myself? In the middle of a dream?' said the dormouse, shocked. 'Don't you know that's the surest way to bring on a nightmare?'

'I do believe the dormouse is still dreaming, even while he's talking to us,' said Robin, smiling and shaking his head.

'Of course I am,' replied the tiny creature. 'And so are others aboard this ark. They're dreaming about a wonderful ending to it all as wistfully as my wife and I are.'

'What others?' said Fern, puzzled. 'All our family and our friends have gone ashore to explore. What others can you mean?'

'There are three who cannot share your happiness,' replied the dormouse, yawning again. 'Like mine and my wife's, their dream is yet to be concluded. But it's back to bed for me, for the River of Dreams still flows ahead as far as the mind's eye can see. Good night . . .' and he snuggled back into his cosy world of imagination.

Robin and Fern turned to look around the now deserted ark. They could see nothing of a 'three' who could not share the happiness of the People.

It wasn't selfishness that made them turn back to watch their family and friends busily settling into the dream valley. Rather, it was because the safety of their own overruled everything else, including themselves. But, in the meantime, Robin and Fern wanted only to bask in the sights and sounds of the joyous People, already beginning to fit their old lives to the new.

The two grannies had hobbled off to set up emergency cooking stations. Behind them came Toadflax and Nettles, carrying the heavy cauldrons and wooden stirring spoons. Already the dim, genius mind of Toadflax was planning a modern kitchen filled with his wonderful inventions. Nettles, burdened with heaped stew bowls, complained bitterly every step of the way to the foot of the oak tree.

'How can I be a deadly archer in Robin's band with wrinkled-up fingers?' he cried, despairingly. 'I want to be a warrior not a cook!'

Finn was wading contentedly in the shallows

of the stream, his sharp harpoon poised to strike. Behind him paddled an adoring Pansy, carrying a reed basket to hold the shoals of silver minnow he would surely catch. Dashing along the bank were Foxglove and Coltsfoot, shouting for Finn to spear to port or starboard each time they spied a flash of silver.

Pimpernel strolled alone, deep in thought. Though he had fought in defence of the People, he had slain his own leader. His guilt went deep, for despite everything, Pimpernel was always a member of the Nightshade Clan. But he knew that wickedness had ruled his clan for a long, long time. Yet there had always been a core of goodness there, among his abused and fearful family. He resolved, during that lonely stroll, to restore the fortunes and good name of his family. Never again would they be cowed and beaten by evil rulers. He, Pimpernel, would rule with kindness to raise up his clan once again. And just down the stream, around the bend, awaited a new oak for a new beginning.

His step quickened, as did his surging, excited hopes for the future.

High on a hill, a trio of serious poets stood on a rocky outcrop, surrounded by a host of golden daffodils. Teasel, Meadowsweet and Quickthorn were gazing around in search of wordy inspiration to honour the paradise the People could now call their own. Just then, Meadowsweet caught sight of Sedge, their faithful water-vole, pottering in perfect peace along the sandy bank far below.

'What an uplifting sight!' she cried. 'I feel a poem coming on,' and she began to quote from her head, her graceful arms and hands fluttering in imitation of Sedge and his family pottering.

> 'See him toil, our noble Sedge,
> Softening more his earthen floor,
> Inviolate in his dark redoubt
> He curls about to spy things out . . .'

'Why can't I end the poem as well as I started,'

she fumed, stamping her foot. 'I know what I want to say but the words just drift away.'

'Don't fret, struggling poetess,' grinned Teasel. 'I'll always be here to snatch up the wisps that waft from your head. I'll end your poem for you. How's this?'

'Close and safe and snugly warm,
And comfortingly oozing—'

'How dare you, Teasel?' cried Meadowsweet, angrily. 'That ending was drifting into my head just as you interrupted. Go away, you tiresome poetry-thief!'

'I'll creep away as humbly as possible,' said Teasel, his grin ever wider. 'You'll find me helping the carpenters, if you need another poetry lesson,' and he ran down the hill to offer the carpenters a strong and willing back.

'Alone with our talents at last,' said Meadowsweet, glancing shyly at Quickthorn, who stood deep in thought, a faraway look in his eyes. It was as if he was gazing at some place only his great mind could see. In a small voice, Meadowsweet went on, 'Perhaps you would quote me a small gem of poetry that I could treasure in my mind for ever, Quickthorn?'

Her hero obliged. In a sad and whispery voice, his young face etched with despair, he uttered the words, 'To be or not to be, that is the question . . .'

'Oh, not questions again,' sighed Meadow-sweet. 'What have silly questions got to do with rhyming? And you were supposed to be a great poet, Quickthorn. I think I'll leave you and your questioning mind on this hill. Perhaps some great work will flood into your head here among the daffodils, though I doubt it. Myself, I have important things to do. Robin has put me in charge of the new library the carpenters are building in our new oak tree,' and she, too, dashed down the hill to supervise the stacking of the books aboard the ark in readiness for their removal to the brand new library.

The busy carpenters were a bit annoyed as she bustled among them, handing their tools and chiding them to work faster. 'The greatness of the Willow Clan is in their history and poetry books,' she declared pompously, 'and I number myself among those poets in the pages. I expect you honest woodworkers have read all my poems to satisfy your love of culture. But I, too, from my lofty heights, am willing to develop horny hands in the name of the People. Hand me an axe, that I might hew among you.'

In fact, Meadowsweet was only there because she wanted to be near Teasel, who was sweating and grinning as he sawed a piece of timber.

This time it was the bird who said it. The magpie scout had just returned to the ark after transferring his family and treasure to a new nest, high in the oak tree. He had no need to shout, for the ark was empty and silent. He said it again to Robin and Fern, who were gazing at and delighting in the activities of their joyous family and friends, now ashore. They were startled by his words.

'It's good that we're all happy at long last,' said the bird. 'At least, nearly all of us. From this perch, I can see three who are nowhere as happy as we.'

'That's the second time three has been mentioned to us two,' said Fern to Robin, bewildered. She looked up. 'Explain the puzzle to us, magpie.'

'From up here, I can see three Human children, looking very lost and miserable,' said the bird.

'Of course, that three,' said Fern, concerned. 'I feel ashamed to have selfishly forgotten about them for so long.'

'We should all feel ashamed,' said Robin, soberly. 'And I do.'

At once, they went to the stern of the ark and looked out along the snaking anchor-line to where the three children were sitting forlornly on the bows of their rowing-boat.

Eighteen

A CRY ACROSS THE CENTURIES

'Forgive us,' pleaded Robin, seeing their sad faces. 'We're so caught up in the excitement of finding our new valley we quite forgot about you.'

'After you shared the disasters and triumphs with us, too,' said Fern. 'We apologise most humbly, dear friends.'

'Come ashore with us,' invited Robin. 'Fern and I will enjoy your company on a stroll through our paradise home. For it belongs as much to you as it does to us.'

'We can't go ashore,' said the friend, simply. 'We've tried, but a strange force seems to stop us leaving the ark or our boat. It's as if something is telling us we don't belong in your valley.'

'You've found your home and we're pleased for you,' said the frightened girl. 'But it's plain we don't belong any more. We three can never share your lives, and now we feel lost and alone, and we just want to go home to the flooded valley of our families and friends.'

'Considering we helped you Willow people a lot, I think it's about time you helped us,' said the boy, loudly. 'I admit I enjoyed the voyage and the adventure, but I've eaten all the stew I can stomach. So, if you'll wave a magic wand and release us from your spell, we can be back home in a jiffy. Frankly, I'm dying for some of my mum's fish and chips. So just return us to our own time and world, and there'll be no hard feelings.'

'I wish we could,' said Robin, helplessly, 'but, as we said before, the People know nothing of magic. We, too, are just ordinary folk swept along by the mysterious forces that rule us. I'm sorry, we wish we could help.'

Just then, help arrived in the practical form of Sedge. Slopping oozy mud all over the deck, he clambered happily aboard and listened as the problem of the Human children was explained to him. He pondered awhile then spoke.

'As I recall, the Human children became a part of our lives when a bond was formed between us. That bond was the anchor-line, which still stretches between our lives and theirs. The line is a thread that binds their time to ours.'

'So what's the solution, Sedge?' asked Robin, mystified.

'What does your wisdom tell us?' asked anxious Fern.

'That, for the Human children to return to

their own world, they must sever the bond between us,' said Sedge. He leaned from the bow of the ark, and shouted to the three lost souls in the boat. 'Take up the swords you used so valiantly during the battle for the ark against the Nightshade gang. Then together, and with all your strength, strike through the anchor-line that binds us. Strike hard. Good luck and goodbye.'

And the girl, the boy and the friend raised their sharp swords above their heads and brought them slashing down. As the anchor-line parted, the sound of Robin's goodbye and Fern's good-bye, and the croaked goodbye from the magpie, rang in their ears as they fell dizzily into deep unconsciousness . . .

'This is madness,' yelled the boy above the howling wind. 'What are we doing chasing a stupid log across the flood in a storm?'

'Let me try with the anchor-line once more,' implored the girl. 'I'm sure I'll snag it this time. We're so near, just let me try again,' and she hurled it for the third time. It bit and, for some strange moments, the three children felt as if they were a part of the log they had chased for so long, oblivious to the danger of the heaving waters. But the tension and strain were too much: the claws of the anchor tore free from the log and fell into the sea.

'They were shouting goodbye,' cried the girl, despairingly. 'You heard them as clearly as I did.'

'Wind can play tricks in your ears,' said the boy, though uneasily. 'It makes all kinds of weird sounds when you're frightened – as I am. Let's turn this boat round and row for the shore before we're all drowned.'

The girl had to agree, though reluctantly. They were, indeed, in danger of being washed overboard if they stayed any longer.

As the boys began to row hard for the shore and the twinkling lights of home she gazed back longingly. Was it only in her imagination that she could dimly see a strange-looking log, bearing ramshackle sails, disappearing into the mists and spray of the storm? Had she dreamed of a quest in search of a valley that lay at the end of the River of Dreams?

She glanced down at the slopping water in the bottom of the boat. Floating amid the debris, she saw tiny scraps of bright green cloth and slivers of wood that vaguely resembled tiny swords. Her head swirling, she looked around and noticed a fishing catapult clumsily positioned on the bows of the rowing-boat, and a wrenched-open locker spilling hooks, lead-shot and floats about the sodden planking floor.

As the boat neared the shore the friend made a remark. 'Those weird sounds, or the wind we heard,' he said. 'Say I'm daft, but they sounded so familiar . . . like voices I'd heard before.'

'I liked Sedge very much,' said the boy, softly. So softly that he was really talking to himself.

'If the whole thing was a dream, then I'm still dreaming now,' cried the girl. 'And I'll relive that dream till the end of my days.'

'I think we all will,' said the friend, as the rowing-boat coasted into the shore. 'But a dream we will never share with others.'

'Not likely!' said the boy, stoutly. 'If I sailed on a quest on an ark to find the end of the River of Dreams, that's my business. It's not the kind of thing I'd talk about at school. I'll keep quiet if you two promise to as well.'

'I will,' said the friend.

'So will I,' said the girl, though wistfully.

Before they left the flooded shore to return and face the music from their angry parents at home, they turned once more to gaze out across the now calming waters . . .

It was not fancy that they heard the voices on the wind again.

'Goodbye, Human children, remember us . . .'

'We'll never forget you, Willow Clan,' wept the girl, her arms spread wide towards the sea.

'Nor ever will we,' murmured the two boys as they led the sobbing girl home.

And even when they were grown-up and living

unadventurous Human lives of boredom and sameness, they never did.

And far away, in another time, a valley and a stream echoed to the sound of joy and laughter as the People went about their undisturbed lives. The circle was completed, the dream of the Willow Clan and all of their friends realized . . .

Welcome home . . .

hODDER

Another Hodder Children's Book

If you have enjoyed this book, look out for other books by W.J. Corbett

THE BATTLE OF CHINNBROOK WOOD

W. J. Corbett

The Dingles belongs to the kids of Chinnbrook Wood: a wild place of ancient rivalries.

Many a battle's been fought for possession of the old stone bridge at its heart – a treasury of secrets and hidden legends . . .

But now a fearsome enemy threatens The Dingles. A new battle looms . . . And it calls for something unexpected from archrivals Val and Joe . . .

A Gift Book from Hodder Children's Books

THE DRAGON'S EGG AND OTHER STORIES

W.J. Corbett

Kicking through the autumn leaves at the bottom of his garden, George uncovers a large pair of nostrils. Burrowing deeper, he discovers a large dragon, blinking, as if emerging from a very deep sleep.

As George listens to the dragon's story, he is drawn into a fantastic, enchanted world. A world of wicked dragons and weak dragons, greedy dragons and gentle dragons, a world that could be imaginary, but could be very, very real . . .

A Story Book from Hodder Children's Books

HAMISH

W.J. Corbett

Hamish is a mountain goat.

All his friends are mountain goats. The only trouble is – Hamish is terrified of climbing mountains.

Every day his friends clatter off to seek adventure in the high hills, and every day Hamish makes more excuses to stay behind in the comfort of his heathery bed.

Until one day, Hamish hears a cry for help – and only he can save the day . . .